THE
MULLIGANS
of MT. JEFFERSON

Other books by Don Reid:

Heroes and Outlaws of the Bible

Sunday Morning Memories

You Know It's Christmas When ...
(with Debo Reid and Langdon Reid)

The Statler Brothers: Random Memories
(with Harold Reid)

O Little Town

One Lane Bridge TB

Piano Days "

✳

donreid.net

THE
MULLIGANS
of MT. JEFFERSON

A NOVEL

DON REID

David C Cook®

transforming lives together

THE MULLIGANS OF MT. JEFFERSON
Published by David C Cook
4050 Lee Vance View
Colorado Springs, CO 80918 U.S.A.

David C Cook Distribution Canada
55 Woodslee Avenue, Paris, Ontario, Canada N3L 3E5

David C Cook U.K., Kingsway Communications
Eastbourne, East Sussex BN23 6NT, England

David C Cook and the graphic circle C logo
are registered trademarks of Cook Communications Ministries.

This story is a work of fiction. All characters and events are the product of the author's imagination. Any resemblance to any person, living or dead, is coincidental.

LCCN 2011941024
ISBN 978-1-4347-6494-2
eISBN 978-1-4347-0488-7

© 2012 Don Reid
Published in association with The Seymour Agency,
475 Miner Street Road, Canton, NY 13617

The Team: Don Pape, Steve Parolini, Amy Kiechlin,
Nick Lee, Caitlyn York, Karen Athen
Cover Design: GearBox Design
Cover Photo: iStockphoto

Printed in the United States of America
First Edition 2012

1 2 3 4 5 6 7 8 9 10

102911

This one is from my heart to my boys,
Debo and Langdon.
… good sons make good fathers …

mul´-li-gan: n. a do-over; a free shot given a golfer when the previous shot was poorly played; also a stew of meat and vegetables.

CHAPTER ONE

MT. JEFFERSON, VIRGINIA
1959

Lt. Buddy Briggs was lying in bed next to his wife. On the nightstand, the clock radio Amanda had given him for Christmas two years ago said it was 5:16 a.m. It kept pretty good time for a dime-store special. In exactly fourteen minutes the alarm would go off under the guise of a radio show, and Crazy Charlie's Coffee Pot would fill the room with a weather report, baseball scores, Khrushchev, and Connie Francis. Should he wait for the alarm and hope for a few more minutes of sleep, or just get up and get it over with?

"Are you awake?"

"I am now," Amanda said with a sleepy smile in her voice.

"Sorry. But I was just lying here thinking about Shirley Ann and the baby. Are you going to call her this morning or wait to hear from her?"

"If we don't hear something by eight, I'll call her. But don't worry now. She's in good hands."

"I know that. But those pains she was having last night ... If the baby comes soon, how early would it be?"

"The baby is due July twentieth. And today is what?"

"Wednesday."

"I know *that*, silly." She kicked him playfully under the sheets.

"Wednesday, June seventeenth."

"So that would mean it's four more weeks and a few days to full term. She'll be okay. They'll be okay."

"I still find it hard to believe that our sixteen-year-old daughter ..."

"Seventeen!" she corrected him.

"Okay, seventeen-year-old daughter is about to be somebody's mother."

"And you, old man, are about to be somebody's grandpa."

"Don't be so smug because you know that makes you ..."

"Yeah, what does that make me?"

"That makes you the prettiest grandmother I've woken up next to ... in weeks."

"Okay, big boy, I can kick harder than that last one."

"What? I said you were the prettiest—"

The ring of the phone stopped him in midsentence. Nothing is louder or more unsettling than a screaming telephone after bedtime or before breakfast. But as a police officer with the Mt. Jefferson force, he had learned to be a little less alarmed each time it rang. It was rarely good news, but it was almost always business. However, this morning—Shirley Ann weighed heavily on his mind—it could be personal. He reached for the receiver and picked it up in the middle of the second ring.

"Hello."

The pause after the initial hello was so long that Amanda sat up in bed, wide awake, so she could see the expression on his face. There was none. He was listening intently. It scared her that he wasn't writing anything on the pad that always lay on the nightstand next to a pencil ready for middle-of-the-night note taking. Names and addresses were hurriedly scratched down before he would leap out of bed and jump into clothes that he invariably put out the night before for just such emergencies.

Amanda put her hand on his arm and quietly said, "What is it?" but he only shook his head slightly and kept listening. He finally said, "I'll be right there" and then placed the phone back in its cradle.

He looked at her and said, "Harlan has been shot."

"Oh, no! Harlan? What happened?"

"Intruder. At his house. Just a few minutes ago. He's on his way to the hospital." But Buddy Briggs still wasn't moving. He lay back down and exhaled as if a bad day was just ending instead of beginning. Harlan Stone was one of the closest friends he had in the world.

"Should I go with you to be with Darcy and the boys? They're all okay, aren't they?" Amanda asked.

"Yeah. They're okay."

"How bad is it, Buddy? And I dread asking you that because I don't want to hear it."

"He's alive. But how bad? I'm not sure. Nobody is yet. That's where I'll go first. To the hospital. Then I'll let you know."

"I'll go with you."

"No. You stay here in case Shirley Ann calls. You may wind up at the hospital anyway if the baby comes early."

He closed his eyes, and she rubbed his arm.

"Before I go, I need to call Cal," Buddy said more to himself than to Amanda.

But before he could reach for the phone, a sudden loud voice startled them. "This is Crazy Charlie and it's raging hot and the ole coffee pot is steaming and screaming and you lazy heads better get out of bed cause it's five thirty-one and that lucky ole sun ..."

Buddy slammed his fist hard on the Off button and dressed quickly in silence.

Amanda was at the counter pouring herself a cup of coffee when he walked past her and stopped at the kitchen phone on the wall. She knew, without looking, the number he was dialing. She could faintly hear Cal answer at the Methodist parsonage and then Buddy say, "Harlan has been shot. I'm on my way to the hospital. Meet me there."

CHAPTER TWO

The first memory they all had of their triangular friendship was from the fifth grade. Cal Vaxter and Harlan Stone had been next-door neighbors since their births in the same year and the same month. They were best friends, and their fathers were both downtown merchants, which put their families in the same circles socially and economically. They had shared most of the same teachers through elementary school, and in that fifth year, under the tutelage of Miss Eleanor Patterson, they sat side by side in desks on the back row. Miss Eleanor's impending deafness had protected them from being blamed for most of the disruptions they were guilty of and had occasionally brought them undeserved glory when she praised them for a wrong answer they convinced her she hadn't heard correctly. That fateful meeting with their third vertex on the playground at lunch recess was the beginning of another chapter of their lives and legendary brotherhood.

For reasons now lost to the ages, Cal and Harlan had become embroiled in a disagreement with four disgruntled sixth-graders. Years later they tried to remember if the boys had stolen their marbles or were upset because they had whistled at one of their girlfriends. Either way, they were into serious name-calling and then pushing and shoving and finally slaps and knocks. About the time one of the upperclassmen put a fist to Harlan's lip and he tasted blood and Cal found himself on the ground with three on top of him, a strange boy of grace came out of the gathering crowd and started slinging bodies in all directions. In thirty seconds the fight was won or conceded, depending on who was telling the story, and new friendships had been forged.

"What's your name?"

"Buddy."

"Buddy Briggs? I've heard of you."

"You in Miss Weller's class?"

"Yeah."

"Thanks for helpin' us out. But I had 'em on the run."

"Yeah." Buddy laughed. "You had all three of them on the run. All you had to do was turn over and you'd have been on top of them."

They all three laughed at this and not for the last time. They would recall and laugh at this chance meeting many times through many years. That day they rode their bikes home from school and discovered that Buddy lived only six blocks over. And six blocks was as far away from one another as they ever were ... until the war separated them.

An ambulance and police cars with flashing lights were parked at the emergency-room door as Buddy pulled up and stopped. He left his car in the circular drive and ran inside. He stopped at the desk for an update.

"Briggs. I'm with the police department," he said to the tall, heavyset woman whose name tag told him she was Nurse Hendricks.

"I know who you are," she shot back with something between annoyance and business-as-usual. "You're here for the Stone situation."

"Yes. What's the latest?"

"He's here. Only been here a few minutes, though. He's in the OR, and they're prepping him for surgery."

"Which operating room?"

"That shouldn't matter to you right now because you can't go back there."

"I thought you said you knew who I was."

"I do, Mr. Briggs. But here, *I'm* the authority. And no one can go back there until a doctor says so." As an afterthought she added, "You're not family, are you?"

Buddy decided he was not going to answer any more of her questions. He walked briskly around the reception desk toward the double doors that led to the inner halls of the hospital when someone from behind called his name.

"Buddy!"

"Hey, Cal."

"What in the world has happened?"

"I just got here myself. Looks like Harlan has been shot, and I don't have much more than that. I don't know where and I don't know how bad."

"I could tell you that if you had bothered to ask." It was Nurse Hendricks again.

Buddy just looked her in the eye and waited for her to continue. Consulting a file in her hand, she did.

"Mr. H. Stone was wounded in the left side. Bleeding was minimal. No record yet of organ damage or the severity of the wound itself. He is presently in the operating room awaiting Dr. Sidney Yandell, who is in the building, or Dr. Paxton, who is the surgeon on call. The patient is conscious and alert and in substantial pain. What else do you need to know?"

"I need to know why you didn't tell me all this earlier," Buddy said with rising anger in his voice.

Ignoring him completely, the nurse looked at Cal Vaxter and said, "Are you family?"

"I'm the family minister."

"Then *you* can go back."

Cal looked at Buddy, and Buddy glared at Nurse Hendricks for a brief second and said, "I tell you what, ma'am. We're both going back, and if you don't like that, call the cops."

HARLAN STONE

CHAPTER THREE

Harlan Briscane Stone always knew what was expected of him. He didn't come from privilege, but he came from enough money to take privilege for granted. His father had instilled that in him from the day of his birth. Never telling him he was better than anyone else, but always telling him no one was better than he was. H. V. Stone had earned his money, every dime of it, through long hard hours of work, if you let him tell it. Others in Mt. Jefferson may have had a different take on how he acquired the considerable wealth he had hoarded away in all three of the city's banks, but no one could call him a crook. And certainly not to his face, because he owed no man and took no time in telling this to anyone he would meet or talk to in a day's time. H. V. Stone was a backslapper, a glad-hander, and a salesman of the highest order. He sold not just himself, but a product that could be bought nowhere else in the city limits. He had a lock on the market, a lock on the town, and a lock on his family. A family that consisted of his wife, Esther, and his only child, Harlan. And Harlan Stone grew up always knowing what was expected of him.

H. V. and Esther were the ideal couple in their social circle and the perfect parents in the eyes of all who cared to take notice. It was only in the privacy of their modest home on Corbin Street that their disagreements were aired. Or make that just "disagreement." Because the only thing they ever argued about was the neighborhood. They lived so far below their means that Mrs. Stone couldn't let a three-day period pass without making some comment about building a new home or moving to a bigger house or just living in a little more style than they did. But H. V. counted his wealth in numbers and required little when it came to the niceties of life. He didn't care what his house looked like or what the houses around him looked like. He lived in a middle-class neighborhood, but that was already so much more than what he'd been used to while growing up. The roof didn't leak, and the yard was big enough for a dog. He had no intention of spending good money on such useless things as a bigger house and a newer car. Esther would have to learn that money in the bank was just that—money in the bank. That's where money belonged, and that's where it would go each week and each year as long as he lived and controlled the books of his business. The source of the cash that just kept rolling in was a little store on the corner of Augusta and Main, elegantly named Stones by Stone Jewelers. The cleverness of this mouthful of a title was lost on the local citizenry, and everyone simply referred to it as Stone's.

Stone's was where you bought the little silver spoons for the baby showers and the starter bracelets for her sixth birthday. Stone's was where you shopped for the gold chain and cross for his confirmation and the friendship ring for that steady girlfriend. Stone's was where the nervous young men would gangle in and search for just the right size and right price tag, for the diamond that would adorn her finger for the rest of her *life, and then return with the young bride-to-be to pick out wedding bands. And Stone's was where you would naturally be drawn to for all of her birthdays, anniversaries, and Christmases. Stone's carried sterling silver and pewter and all things shiny, but without question, it was a gold mine.*

Harlan B. Stone always knew what was expected of him. He knew from the time he was a child that he was to get good grades, show good manners, play football, marry a nice local girl, and take care of the family business.

"Now, son, I want you to play football when you get to MJHS. You hear me?"

"I hear you, Poppa. I'm going to kick the ball farther than anybody ever has."

"That's my boy. And you're going to run. That's going to be your talent. Run every day and everywhere you go. Build up those muscles, and you'll be the fastest there ever was."

"I'll win a scholarship. You wait and see."

"You don't need a scholarship, son. Let some of those other boys have that scholarship fund. We'll take care of college. Don't you worry about that."

And he didn't. Harlan never worried about anything for the first fifteen years of his life. He made the good grades that were expected from him. He learned the good manners that were required of him and used them on his teachers to his best advantage. And he excelled in everything he attempted. President of his class, captain of the football team, not to mention the best halfback Mt. Jefferson High ever turned out—and he was voted Most Likely to Succeed in the Aerie, MJH's yearbook. He accomplished everything he set out to do and then set his goals for the

University of Virginia. He would play football for the Cavaliers. His daddy told him he would, so it had to be true. His daddy never lied to him. His mother stayed quietly in the background through all those years and firmly added, "Keep up those grades, Harlan."

Whatever he became in life, Harlan always knew it was what his daddy demanded and what his mother allowed.

CHAPTER FOUR

A second nurse stopped them on their way to the operating room. She was a little older and a little gentler than the one at the desk.

"Hi, Buddy, Cal. Are you both here to see Harlan?"

"Yes, we are."

"You don't remember me do you? We went to school together. Kathy Foster?"

"Sure, Kathy. How are you?" Cal said with a smile even though he couldn't recall ever seeing her before. Buddy made no move to put her at ease with a lie. He only stared at her and waited for her explanation as to why she had stopped them.

"I was Kathy Painter then. But anyway, you'll have to wait just a minute till I can get you each a surgical gown. You'll have to put it on over your clothes before you go in the OR."

But just as she was returning with the attire, another nurse tapped Buddy on the arm.

"Lieutenant, Mrs. Stone is in the lobby. She came over in the police car. She's pretty upset and says she wants to see you."

"Okay. I'll be right there."

Kathy Painter Foster had just given them each a white, ankle-length cotton gown. Buddy handed his back to her.

"Cal, you go on in and see Harlan. I'll go talk to Darcy and see if I can calm her down."

"Fine. I'll be out to see her shortly. I don't figure they'll let me stay long. Hopefully the doctor is here and nearly ready to start."

"He is," Nurse Foster said to Cal as she led him through the double doors. "He should be ready in just a few minutes."

Darcy Stone was sitting in a straight-back chair in the empty waiting area. Her eyes were red and swollen, and she was staring blankly ahead as if seeing nothing and no one. She looked even smaller than her five-foot-two frame. She was still pretty, even with her pale skin and ruffled hair. She stood and hugged Buddy a long time before saying anything.

"I love him so much, Buddy."

"I know you do. Do you feel like talking?"

"I talked to the other officers at the house and all the way over here. I don't know if I have the strength to talk anymore."

"Henry," Buddy yelled to the officer on the door, "get us two coffees, please." He looked back to Darcy and sat her down with his hand on her shoulder before sitting beside her.

"I know it's hard, but tell me everything and exactly the way it happened."

Rubbing her hands and periodically her stomach and the top of her thighs, Darcy spoke slowly and distinctly.

"It must have been around five o'clock. We both heard something in the kitchen. Harlan got up to go see what it was, and I went right behind him. It sounded like—I don't know—a thud or something. Like somebody had pushed in the back door. Nothing breaking or anything like that. Just sort of a thud. When we got to the kitchen door from the hallway, we both saw him. He was hunched over like he was looking for something to hide behind, but he was right there in the middle of the floor. I think I screamed, and Harlan said something like, 'What's going on here? Who are you?'"

And then she began to cry again.

"That's okay. Take your time. The coffee's here."

"Harlan said, 'Who are you?' and then he mumbled something, and I couldn't tell what he was saying."

"Who mumbled something? Harlan?"

"No. The guy. And that's when Harlan picked up a kitchen chair and threw it at him. He kind of ducked, and that was when I first saw the gun. My heart just stopped, and I couldn't move. The next thing I heard was a shot. Sort of a pop. But then my ears started ringing, and I knew it must have been louder than it sounded. And Harlan sort of stumbled back against the kitchen table like he'd tripped over something. I wasn't sure what had happened. I grabbed him to keep him from falling, and the guy just ran out the door."

"What did he look like?"

"I don't know. He had on a mask."

"A mask? What kind of mask?"

"You know, a thing that covered his face."

"Like a Lone Ranger mask, or one that covered his whole head?"

"No. Not his whole head. It was a Halloween mask. Looked like a clown or something."

"But you saw his skin?"

"His skin? What do you mean?"

"The color of his skin."

"Oh. He was white. Dark complexion. Dark hair."

"How tall?"

"I'm not sure. Like I said, he was sort of bent over."

"What did his voice sound like?"

"I told you I couldn't understand what he said."

"I know you couldn't understand his words. I just mean his voice. Was it high pitched or gravelly or young or old?"

"I'm not sure. Just kind of normal I guess. I'm not very much help, am I? Have you been in to see Harlan?" And then she started to cry again.

"No. Cal is back there with him right now."

"I've got to go back and see him. He was talking and everything when they carried him out on the stretcher. But I've got to go back and see him."

"What about the twins? Where are they?"

"Boy Scout camp. They're there for the whole week. Thank God they weren't at home. Can I go back?"

"Not yet. Tell me about the gun. What did it look like?"

"What do you mean?"

"Was it a pistol or a rifle?"

"It was a pistol."

"Do you know the difference between a revolver and an automatic?"

Darcy shook her head and hugged her arms tighter as if she was trying to get warm.

Buddy rubbed his face and took a long swig of his coffee. He had more questions, but he could sense she was out of answers. And until she knew her husband was going to be all right, she was in no shape to concentrate on the information he had to get from her. He put his arm around her and did the only thing either of them could do at this point. He waited.

CHAPTER FIVE

He dated a lot of girls in his teens, but never anyone he was really serious about. He and Cal and Buddy often triple-dated—they went to movies and softball games in the summer and basketball games in the winter. They all went to the prom their junior and senior years, but the only girl who was a part of all of these adventures was Buddy's steady, Amanda Peers. Even on the nights Harlan and Cal didn't have dates, they would tag along with Buddy and Amanda to go eat or go skating at RollerLand. Amanda knew most of the girls Harlan went out with, though she didn't necessarily approve of or like all of them. There were lots of girls from MJHS and some from the neighboring county schools. She and Buddy and Cal used to laugh at how, just when they got to know one of Harlan's girls, he'd show up with a new one. This fed the reputation he was building in school and in town. But everybody loved him or admired him—even the girls he wouldn't date and the guys he stole girls from. While H. V. Stone only thought he was everybody's friend, Harlan Stone really was. Both could sell themselves in a split second with a simple flash of a smile.

Football season was over their senior year, and spring was coloring the valleys of Virginia a bright, deep green. The three stars of the gridiron decided they would try out for the baseball team. They hadn't done that since their freshman year, and they thought it would be fun. Coach Randolph was thrilled to have them, as they were three of the best athletes in the entire school. He had been trying to get them back on the baseball field for three years with no success, and with their renewed interest he saw a chance to finally win a regional title if not a state title. Cal Vaxter was his starting pitcher, and Harlan and Buddy were perfect on the hot corners of first and third. But it was their hitting ability he was counting on for the big payoff. With the training and muscles these guys had developed for football, they would be his third, fourth, and fifth-place hitters for sure in every game. But these sweet dreams and big plans culminated in an unexpected, pre-season visit from H. V. Stone. When he knocked on the door of Coach Bill Randolph's tiny office just off the main floor of the gym, it was obvious what the tenor of the meeting was going to be.

"Mr. Stone."

"Coach, how in the world are you?"

"Just fine, sir. Come on in, and I'll try to find you a place to sit. I've got magazines and ball equipment all over this place."

"That's quite all right, young man. Those are the tools of your trade. The brushes with which you create your art. And you do know that what you do is art, don't you? Just as sure as if that ball field out there is a canvas and you're the master creating a beautiful painting with each one of those players being your colors. You stir them and mix them and then place them where you want them, and in the end, you have a magnificent, winning piece of art."

"Well. I guess that's one way of looking at it."

"It's the only way. And you're the right man for the job. You know the game from the inside out. I used to watch you play for the Mt. Jefferson Eagles. You were some catcher. And the catcher is the soul of the team. The pitcher is the star; the best hitter is the hero; but the catcher—he holds it all together and makes it a team. You were the best, Billy. You were the best."

"Well, thank you, sir. I certainly enjoyed those years playing ..."

"And you're a good coach, too."

"Thank you. I don't ..."

"You know what I think? I think you're going to have a winning season this year. You've got the Vaxter boy. Good arm. Tireless and strong. You've got Briggs on third, and there's nothing going to get past that boy. You don't even need a shortstop with him at third. And, of course, Harlan at first. He's got a glove like flypaper. Shoot, Coach, you won't even need an outfield when those three boys get through with a batter."

Coach Randolph didn't make an attempt to answer or acknowledge the last statement. H. V. Stone never let anyone say anything until he said whatever it was he came to say, and he was just getting started.

"Of course, I'll be honest with you, Billy. Football is my game. It's the real man's game. Hard and rough and real. Blood and flesh mixed in with grass by the time a game is over, to where you can't tell what's red and what's green. That's a real game. And that's what I've always wanted for my boy. Harlan is a football player. This thing with baseball, he's just fooling around. Having some fun. But he's in your hands. And I don't want him hurt. He's going to play for Virginia come fall, and I don't want some crazy kid with a wild arm throwing balls at his head. A man's head is no match for a baseball, Billy. I don't want him sliding in

to a base and messing up knee joints and ankles. In other words, I don't want him messed up in some boy's game so it would hinder him in a real man's game of football next fall. Do you get my drift?"

"I think there's a lot more chance of getting hurt ... "

"Playing football? Of course, there is, Billy. But it's also more honorable. If somebody's going to take my boy out, let it be a man with muscle. He can handle any other boy his age and size on personal contact. And if he doesn't, then, as I said, there's some honor in injury. But just between you and me, Coach, don't let my son get hurt diddling around on the baseball diamond. You hear what I'm saying?"

"I hear you, Mr. Stone."

"I'm no fool, Coach. I know that was a noncommittal answer. You didn't say you understood or that you agree with me. And when I leave, you can justify yourself by saying all you admitted to was that you heard me. But that's okay. You have to leave a man a little room for dignity, I always say. Don't you, Billy? Well, I guess I better get back to work. I got my own kind of diamonds to take care of. Somebody might be looking for a diamond necklace before the day's over, and I certainly don't want to miss any opportunities. Good to see you, Coach, and I hope you have a winning season."

Harlan never knew about his father's visit to the coach's little office off the corner of the gym floor. Billy Randolph never told anyone except his wife, over the dinner table that night. He considered talking to the athletic director but thought better of it and kept the conversation and all the feelings it commanded in him to himself. He played Harlan Stone the way he had always meant to play him. He played every inning and went to bat as many times as possible in every game. Billy showed him no favors and his father no respect. He prayed before every contest that *no boy on either team would see injury during the game, and in the five years he had steered the varsity team, his players had gotten only minor scrapes and bruises. The only time Billy even let himself think about H. V. Stone was when he would spot him in the stands and sometimes when he would close his eyes at night to go to sleep. The words the old man had said to him never bothered him all that much. It was the words he never said back to him that haunted him most.*

CHAPTER SIX

Coach Randolph was two games from a regional title and graduation was less than two weeks away, and he knew if he could just keep the six seniors he had on his first string focused for ten more innings of high school baseball, he could put the trophy in the glass gym case and the contract for another two years of coaching in his desk drawer. The home-field advantage for the Eagles was a plus, and a three-run lead in the top of the fourth meant they could get four more turns at the plate if they needed it. Billy Randolph was thankful for the high school rule of seven-inning games because he just knew his heart couldn't take anymore. The excitement of winning had proved more stressful to him than the previous losing years. Out of the corner of his eye, as he watched his catcher call time and walk to the mound to confer with Cal Vaxter, he caught the dust of a car coming much too fast through the parking lot. As the dust cloud cleared, all his attention was drawn to the man getting out of the driver's seat. It was city patrolman Ollie Moore. He was walking toward the dugout faster than Billy had ever seen him move; all two hundred and seventy pounds of him nearly running across the gravel walkway with a hand on his holster and the other on his hat to keep the first from flapping and the second from blowing away. He came straight toward where Billy was standing at the side screen by the dugout. He was out of breath, and he kept his voice low.

"Hey, Billy."

"Hey, Ollie. What's the hurry?"

"Where's the Stone boy?"

"In the field. Why? What's wrong?"

"It's his daddy. H. V. He's had a heart attack or a stroke or something. I'm not real sure. But it looks bad."

Coach Randolph looked up to get the umpire's attention to call time but then realized the game was still in a time-out. Ollie Moore and his uniform and his urgent body language had gotten everyone's attention, and they all were looking at the coach and the officer, waiting for a sign or an explanation.

"Harlan," Billy yelled, "come on in."

Harlan Stone jogged slowly toward the two authority figures as the stands and the field fell silent. When he got there, Coach Randolph put his hand on his shoulder and spoke directly and softly in his ear.

"It's your dad. He's at the hospital. You need to go with Ollie."

Harlan Stone, first baseman, running back, playboy of the senior class, asked no further questions. He dropped his glove on the bench and picked up his street shoes and followed Sergeant Moore to the still-idling police car. It was his last moment in the world he had known all his life.

For the little information Ollie Moore—city employee and renowned defender of local law—had, he got it right. His mention of both heart attack and stroke proved prophetic. H. V. Stone had been in his jewelry store at 4:35 that afternoon, standing by one of the glass showcases, leafing through a Time *magazine. Seeing his son's baseball game was not a high priority in his life. He had never missed a football game no matter the weather or the distance, but he had let it be known by his inattentiveness that "this bat-and-ball nonsense" was not a contest he planned on watching with any regularity. So while his son was on the field in regional playoffs, he was minding the store with his longtime underpaid employee Maxine, who was dusting the showcases and looking busy until the next customer came in, and his longtime crony employee Fritz, who was in the back with the jeweler glass in his eye. Fritz did all the repairs and engraving and polishing—anything that could make a ten-dollar piece of merchandise look like a hundred-dollar masterpiece. The little bell above the door had dinged, and H. V. looked up.*

"Mrs. Shanvell. How in the world are you?"

"Oh, middling. Just middling."

"Well, you look like a ray of sunshine to me. How's that no-good husband of yours?"

"He's the very reason I'm here. He has just become an Inside Guardian in his lodge...."

"That would be the Odd Fellows. Well, congratulations to him."

"Thank you, Mr. Stone. So I was wondering what you would have with the Odd Fellows' symbol."

"Oh, I have all kinds of things and can order you even more. We have a lapel pin here with their Triple Links on it. Or I can have that made up for you in a ring. Something gold plated."

"That would be nice. But he doesn't like to wear a ring much. They tend to break him out. I think I like the idea of that lapel pin. Mr. Stone? Are you all right?"

H. V. Stone was suddenly leaning with one elbow on the showcase, his head down. His breathing became audible and labored as he looked up at his frequent and loyal customer and said, "Sure, I'm fine, Mrs. ... ah ... what can I help you with?"

"The lapel pin," Mrs. Shanvell said with a question in her voice.

"Do you have it?"

"Do I have what?"

"The pin. You said you had a pin ... Maxine! I can't think ... get Fritz."

And without another word, he fell to the floor, and Mrs. Shanvell screamed while Maxine ran to get Fritz.

Harlan arrived at the hospital in the police cruiser the same time his mother arrived from their house in her Ford coupe. She grabbed his hand, and they pushed through the doors together. Neither spoke, but they both knew what the other was thinking. But even as well as they knew him, they didn't figure on just how tough a character he was. It was a stroke all right, and three days later he had a heart attack lying in the hospital bed. But even the combination of those two mighty forces couldn't do more than make a dent in the hard-shelled heart and soul that had become H. V. Stone. But that dent was enough to change the lives of the son and wife forever. Herschel Stone wouldn't die, but he would really never again live life as he had become accustomed to living it. And neither would anyone else around him.

CHAPTER SEVEN

His eyes were closed, and his face was pinched with pain. Nurses and attendants were hustling around him, prepping him for the operation. Nurse Kathy walked Cal to the middle of the room—to the white table that was the center of attention. She said quietly to Rev. Cal Vaxter, "I'll come get you when the doctor is ready to start." And then she left the two of them alone.

Cal picked up his friend's limp hand and held it in his. It was cold and rubbery. He instinctively began rubbing it with both his hands as if to bring some warmth back to the white, pallid fingers.

"Harlan. Can you hear me?"

Harlan's eyes opened, and some hint of a smile crossed his lips.

"What are you doing here, Cal? Does this mean I'm going to die?"

"No, they would have sent in a priest for that. I don't do last rites."

Harlan stifled an awkward laugh. And then, smiling through his pain said, "How about confessions. You do those?"

"You still got the wrong boy. Remember I'm Protestant. You got a confession, you can go straight to the Big Guy all by yourself. You don't need me in the middle."

Harlan smiled again. "I won't lie to you, pal. I'm scared."

"That's okay to be scared. I don't think you have any reason to be, but it's okay to admit what you feel. The doctor is on his way and says he can fix you up good as you ever were."

"Um. I was hoping for something better than that. How about something in a thirty-one waist and my old hairline? Maybe like I was in high school."

"He's only a doctor. Not one of the twelve disciples. Although I admit it's going to take a miracle to put you back in shape. And I'm not talking about your body."

Harlan grimaced and squeezed Cal's hand as pain shot through some part of his torso. Then he looked up at him and smiled that big, familiar smile that had gotten him through every storm life ever threw at him. "Let's get the old body fixed for now, and then we'll work on my soul."

"I started working on that years ago, pardner. But right now you need to rest and quit talking."

"Is Buddy here?"

"He's in the waiting room with Darcy."

"Stay close to her, Cal. She's going to need you if I don't make it."

"You're going to make it. So get those thoughts out of your head. But I can't stay. Here comes the nurse who's going to tell me to get out of here. I'll be right outside with Buddy and Darcy, and we'll all be praying for you. And it wouldn't hurt for you to do that for yourself."

And with the most sincere look on his face—one Cal had never seen—Harlan looked at him and said, "Do you think I don't?"

"I think you do a lot more than you admit. Now don't talk anymore. They're motioning for me to get out. I'll see you in the recovery room."

"Thanks, pal. Thanks for coming."

Cal released his grip on his friend's hand, but Harlan wouldn't let go. He lay there with his eyes closed, gripping harder with each passing second. Cal didn't move until Kathy Foster came and took the patient's hand and nodded to the preacher that it was time to leave.

In the waiting room, Cal sat down on the other side of Darcy, and they hugged.

"How is he? Can I see him?"

"Not yet. Dr. Yandell came, and they've started surgery. But I talked to him, and he was doing just fine. Where are the boys?"

"Boy Scout camp. I hate to call them so early."

"Yes, let's wait for that. He's going to be okay."

Buddy nodded in agreement. And he and Cal made eye contact over Darcy's head.

CHAPTER EIGHT

Darcy Brennaman had not been a part of Harlan Stone's high school life. She grew up on a large farm several miles outside of Mt. Jefferson and attended a county school. Her only contact with MJH was when her school, Harrison High, played them in a sports competition. She knew who Harlan was by reputation and admired him from a distance on occasion, but their eyes had never met. She had shopped at Stone's with her mother all of her life and had gone in to pick out a special graduation necklace from her grandparents just days before her commencement exercise. But she never saw Harlan there. Her main remembrances of him involved the football field or the baseball diamond. But to him she was only a girl in the bleachers until that day at the post office. That was the summer after they graduated from their respective alma maters, but so much had happened in Harlan's life before their fateful meeting.

When H. V. Stone's only child walked down the aisle to get his diploma that third of June, it was supposed to be the stepping stone

*to greater things. The University of Virginia. A starting position on
the Cavaliers football team. An education that was never afforded
to H. V. but that would make his son the first in the Stone line to
be a college man. H. V. had planned for and looked forward to this
day since he first held his boy in his arms in the maternity ward
of Lenity General Hospital. And how ironic that this very hospital
was where he would lie alone as his seventeen-year-old son walked
across the gymnasium stage that night in a cap and gown. Esther
had offered to stay with him, but he had insisted she go watch their
son graduate. She gave little resistance, and he knew she wanted to
be there as much as he did. But the even sadder fact that preyed on
his mind in his lonely, stark room was what his illness and inability
was doing to the two people he loved most in the world. The doctors
told him he might never be able to resume the work schedule he had
enjoyed all his life. He knew in the deepest recesses of his mind, just
by looking at the dark, sunken eyes of his once lovely wife, that she
was not capable of taking the reins for the sake of the family. He put
his hands over his eyes in an effort to block out reality. He couldn't
stand to let in the thoughts that were prying at his conscience. There
was only one person to take over the business, and in his aching
heart he knew it.*

*None of this was ever discussed. Harlan graduated that night
and partied with his friends into the a.m. hours, and then the next
morning at eight thirty, he was in front of the store, under the sign
Stones by Stone Jewelers, sweeping the sidewalk in his shirtsleeves.
He spoke to a few other neighboring merchants, accepted their
congratulations, and thanked them for asking about his dad—and
then at eight forty-five he went back inside, put on his suit coat,*

opened the cash register, turned on the lights in all the glass cases, and began the business day as usual.

"Hello, Harlan. Good to see you. How's your dad doing?"

"He's doing much better, thank you. Just taking it day by day."

"Do you think he'll ever come back to work?"

"That'll be up to him and his doctor. But we can take care of anything you might be looking for. What is it I can help you with?"

"Harlan, I really like that necklace, but your daddy always gave me a twenty-percent discount on everything I bought. And I've bought a lot of jewelry from him through the years."

"I know you have, Mr. James. And I'm going to take care of you just like he did. I've already given you your usual twenty percent with that price right there. But I'll give you thirty percent off if you decide to take the earrings that match the necklace."

"*Good morning, young man. I'm George Hanson with Stottlemeyer Wholesale Jewelry. I've been making calls on this store for over fifteen years. Is Mr. Stone in?*"

"*Yes, he is. I'm Mr. Stone.*"

"*Not the Mr. Stone I've been dealing with.*"

"*No sir. But I'm the one you'll be dealing with now. What can I do for you? And why don't you show me the good catalog you have in the car instead of this overpriced one you have in your hands and save us both some time?*"

The coach from UVA wrote and phoned a number of times that summer, as did the registration office. But Harlan never took the calls or answered the letters, and to his knowledge, neither did his father. Esther divided her time between the hospital and the store, and after H. V. came home, she was seen less and less in the store or any other place about town. The routines changed drastically for all three of them, but in silence they each accepted their fate and lived quietly with the lives they had inherited. Some of the town pitied them; some admired them; a few even offered to help them; but they all were talking about them. And that just made Stone's even more of a local landmark. If business was the bottom line, then business was good.

The new Mr. Stone didn't just learn the jewelry business—the business became a part of his breathing. Like his dad before him, he kept long hours and efficient books. He shook the hands and slapped the backs that kept the flow of traffic coming in the door. He gave discounts that were already figured in the profits to old familiar customers and enticed new ones with the same percentages. Everyone in town would brag about the "good deal" they could get at Stone's, and they weren't lying. Everyone got the same deal, but each one thought theirs was better than the other fellow's. Women liked dealing with Harlan because of his charm and looks, and men liked dealing with him because he was the owner. He worked the floor constantly and spoke individually with each person who walked through the door. He flashed the smile at anyone who even hinted they might want to buy something and encouraged them all to "take their time and feel free to look around." Maxine knew that no matter what her young boss said to the public, she wasn't to leave a potential customer alone for over thirty seconds. That was the Stone way. Appear friendly, but keep the pressure on.

And keep the old employees on. Harlan knew too much change too soon could change the whole dynamic of what had taken his father years to establish; Maxine was always in the front, and Fritz was always in the back. That combination had worked for H. V., and Harlan knew it would work for him. Even though Fritz had never been one of his favorite people, he realized how valuable he was to the operation. Not to mention how close he was to his father.

"Good morning. Stone's Jewelers."

"Harlan, is your father down there again?"

"Hi, Mom. Yes, he is. You want to talk to him?"

"No. I just wanted to make sure where he was. He leaves the house, and I never know where he's going. He shouldn't even be driving."

"I know. But being here makes him happy."

"What does he do? Just sit there in that back room all day?"

"Not all day, usually. But he's here most of it, I guess. He and Fritz sit back there and smoke and talk about the old days. He never comes out even when a customer asks for him. I went back yesterday and told him Bob Conyers was out here and wanted to say hi, and he just waved me off."

"And Bob is one of his oldest friends in the world. And I wish he wouldn't smoke like he does. With a stroke and a heart attack, he's going to kill himself yet."

"Mom, we can't stop that. I think sometimes that's why he does it. I've talked to him, but I haven't had any luck."

"Well, talk to him again, son. He just walks away from me. See what you can do."

"I will."

"And tell him to come home for lunch. I have soup."

"I will."

"Good-bye."

"Good-bye."

CHAPTER NINE

"Hello?"

"Amanda," Buddy said into the phone.

"Oh, thank God. I was hoping you would call soon. What's going on there?" Amanda asked with true concern.

"He's in surgery right now. He was awake and talking to Cal. But, really, we won't know much till he comes out. How about you? What have you heard from Shirley Ann?"

"I called her, and she's doing fine. No pains this morning. Said she was just feeling fat. And she said to tell you hi and that she loved you."

"Every time I think about her living in that little apartment above that garage with that boy, it makes me want to ..."

"That boy, Buddy, is your son-in-law. And he has a name. If you say 'that boy' again to Shirley Ann instead of 'Louis Wayne,' you're just going to make matters worse."

"I'm not going to say it to her. But ..."

"Just don't worry about all that now. Let me handle this end."

"Well, where is that ... Louis Wayne? Is he with her?"

"No. He's already gone to work."

"And you don't think he should be with his wife when she's eight months pregnant?"

"If he had stayed home, you would have said he should be out making a living for them. If he goes to work, you say he should ..."

"Okay, I get the point," Buddy said, resigned.

"I know you do, honey. You just can't always admit it. Remember where you were when I was eight months pregnant? You were on a ship heading for Europe."

"Yeah, thanks to Uncle Sam. But I would have been there if I could have. You know that."

"Of course I know that. But nothing is ever exactly the way we plan it to be and *you* know *that*. This is not our plan, but we have to see it through on their terms. It's their life. Shirley Ann and Louis Wayne's. We'll be here for them when they need us and stay out of their way when they don't."

There was a long silence on the telephone line between the phone booth in the lobby of Lenity General Hospital and the Briggs household. Amanda's words lingered and died before Buddy finally picked up the conversation again.

"Are you that much smarter than I am?"

Amanda laughed.

"No. You say what's on your mind, and I say what's on your heart. You just find it difficult to put your heart's feelings into words. I love you, you big galoot."

Amanda always made him smile—even at the most awkward times.

"Right back at you, girl."

"Now tell me about Harlan. Did you find out any more about what happened?"

"An intruder, like I told you. He had on a mask, and he broke in the back door."

"Oh, no! That scares me just thinking about it."

"Darcy is here if you still want to come on over to the hospital."

"Sure. Tell her I'll be there in about fifteen minutes. Are you going to be there?"

"Probably not. If Cal can be with him when he comes out of recovery, I think I'll go over to their house. We've got an officer on duty over there, and they're combing every inch of the neighborhood. I want to look around the place and see if there's anything to be seen."

"Were they robbed?"

"Well, that's one of the things I'll look for. But right now, according to Darcy, I don't think so."

"Okay. Well, be careful. And I love you."

"Yeah, love you, too."

CHAPTER TEN

How Mt. Jefferson's only jewelry store stayed in business during the worst depression this country had ever experienced was a mystery to all the other businessmen who were losing their shirts, not to mention their socks and pants. Banks were going under; factories were closing; mom-and-pop grocery stores were nowhere to be found. Empty storefronts lined the streets of every city in the U.S., and Mt. Jefferson was no different. And for nearly a decade after Harlan Stone took over the family business, he watched the town's Main Street dwindle to just a few stores per block. The five-and-dime stores stayed. One department store weathered it pretty well, and a local hardware store and a small florist were able to keep their doors ajar if not completely open. A couple of grocery-store chains and two locally owned restaurants, Mulligans and Drakos, fed the prudent needs of the sensible citizenry, and Mt. Jefferson managed to keep itself on the map. The entire state of Virginia was hit with less force in those depression years than most of the other states. There was no steel and automobile production; no major industries to fold around the lives of its citizens. Virginia was producing the sort of necessities that even poverty-stricken folks still had to have, such as food and clothing and a popular product they weren't willing to do without—tobacco. So consequently, the Old Dominion's economic recovery was faster than that of the rest of the country.

And for the same reason that Hollywood flourished during this period, Stone's jewelry store persevered. People needed a little comfort from all the misery, and they tended to find it in a darkened movie theater or in a small piece of jewelry. Harlan adapted with the times and carried a much cheaper line than his dad had carried in the thriving years before. He set up credit plans that allowed his customers to pay as little as fifty cents a week for the engagement and wedding rings they had to have or the watch they needed or the bracelet they just couldn't do without. He didn't make the staggering profits that his father had seen, but he kept his head above the water and the doors firmly open. During this time, Mt. Jefferson went from a one-movie-house town to a two-movie-house town. However, Harlan saw to it that no one opened up a competing jewelry store across or down the street. He controlled it all with charm, hard work, and good business sense.

In 1937, just a few short years after high school graduation, young Harlan Stone was the catch of the town. He had his own white-collar business. He was handsome. Smart. Single—but still making and maintaining the reputation of the cavalier bachelor. The other two-thirds of the triangular friendship had taken off for college. Although they had gone their separate ways, Cal Vaxter and Buddy Briggs would return home often for holidays and seasonal breaks, and the old trio would remain as close as they had always been since childhood.

Nothing had changed at the store. H. V. still came in every day in his suit and tie and sat in the back with old Fritz for hours on end. He came in by the back door and left the same way, and Harlan was usually unaware of his going or coming. H. V.'s stroke had changed more than just his speech, *and his family was forced to live in a constant state of simply waiting for him to die. Esther could see the effect all this was having on her son. His face was as bright and smiling as ever, but his eyes were aging, wavering from sad to dead, sometimes in just a matter of minutes. She knew he needed something more in his life. He needed someone he could share his life and even his sorrows with. Esther prayed that her boy would settle down and find that special someone who could put the light back in his tired, fading eyes.*

The post office on Frederick Street closed its counter at 5:00 p.m. every weekday, but the front door was open all night for letter mailing and for those who rented the mailboxes that lined two walls. It was nearly six one night when Harlan parked by the curb and got out of his two-year-old Ford with a handful of stamped mail in his hand. As he pulled open the large wooden door and stepped inside, he heard a pounding and a shriek—"I can't believe it!" He saw no one but heard the same person scream, "How stupid am I?"

He then stepped forward and around the column that was blocking his view and caught a glimpse of one of the prettiest, sweetest faces he had ever seen in his life. And this was saying a lot, because he had seen and kissed quite a few sweet faces. She was standing by the slot in the wall that said LETTERS and would intermittently slam her hand against the wall and scream another, sometimes unintelligible, sentence. After watching this happen a couple more times and being thoroughly entertained by it each time, he finally exposed the secret of his presence and said, "Excuse me. Is there anything I can do to help?"

The little beauty—and she was only five foot two, was his guess— jumped and glared at him.

"How long have you been standing there?"

"Nearly as long as you have, I think."

"And you find this funny?"

"I find it pretty darn interesting."

"Well, I find it very frustrating, and I don't appreciate you laughing at me."

"I'm not laughing. Here, look. Not anymore. Look how serious I am."

"You really think you're cute, don't you?"

"No, but I will admit I'm curious. What exactly are you doing?"

Tears started to fill her eyes, but she tried hard to explain, in a calm voice, her situation.

"I came in here to mail a letter. Just a simple letter. I also had my car keys in my hand, and when I dropped the letter in, the keys went in, too. And then when I . . . are you laughing at me again?"

"Hey, you have to admit that's pretty funny."

"Well, maybe to you. My car is out front, and my keys are in this slot, and there's no way I can . . . aw, what does it matter? You don't care."

"But I do care. And I can help. First, we'll bang on the door that goes to the back and see if anyone is working back there."

Harlan knocked several times and even called out for someone to open the door. His efforts got no reaction, so he turned to the pretty young woman and said, *"Secondly, we'll slide a note under the door. Go over there and get a piece of paper and a pencil, and leave your phone number for anyone who finds a set of car keys in the morning mail pouch."*

The girl did just as he suggested and came back and handed it to him. Harlan slid the note under the door and even knocked on it one more time to see if he could rouse anyone in the back. When his efforts were again awarded with silence, he turned to her and said, *"And now, thirdly, I'll take you home."*

"I don't even know you."

"Or you can walk."

"You think you're pretty slick, don't you?"

"Mmmm. Let's see. You've accused me of thinking I'm really cute, and now you accuse me of thinking I'm pretty slick. How else do you want to try to offend me before I do you a very nice and gentlemanly favor and offer you a ride home? And I'm only going to offer it one more time."

"Do I have a choice?"

"Sure. You can walk."

"I live in Harrison Springs."

"That's about seven miles. You don't want to walk. And I don't bite. So you're better off taking your chances with me."

"Yeah, I guess so. And I know who you are."

"Do you now? Well, you're one up on me because I don't know who you are. So let's make this an even playing field."

"I'm Darcy Brennaman. I've been in your store."

"Not when I was there, or I'd remember you."

"I've been coming there since I was a little girl. You wouldn't remember me. And I saw you play football a lot. I've seen your picture in the paper."

"But I don't know who you are, so let's go get something to eat so you can tell me as much about you as you know about me."

"I think we'll skip all that and I'll just let you take me home."

The ride to the Brennaman farm in Harrison Springs, which was just outside of Mt. Jefferson, turned out to be a pleasant memory for both of them. They talked about their high school rivalries, some of the same people they knew in town, and her remaining year at the State Teachers College at Radford. When he had driven down the long, shaded gravel driveway that led to the large frame farmhouse encircled by a porch, he stopped and let his engine idle as she opened the door.

"*Thanks. I really appreciate the ride home. Sorry I hollered at you back there,*" Darcy said.

"*That's okay. You're forgiven. You have a phone?*"

"*Yeah.*"

"*Are you going to give me your number so I can call you and we can do this again?*"

"*I'm not sure.*"

"*What do you mean you're not sure? I told you I don't bite, and I didn't, did I?*"

Darcy laughed. "*No, but I've heard a lot about you. You've got a lot of girlfriends.*"

"*Wrong. I don't have a single girlfriend right now.*"

"*Right now. Yeah, right. I'll think about it.*"

"*When? You know I know where you live. I could just come out here and sit till you come out of the house, and then you'd have to see me.*"

"*You wouldn't do that.*"

"*Don't bet on it.*"

"*My daddy would probably shoot you.*"

"*I've been shot at before. Phone number?*"

"*How about I'll call you if I decide. I know how to find you. You're at Stone's.*"

"*Suit yourself.*"

And as she got out and closed the door, she said through the open window, "*Thanks again. You're very nice, even though I've heard a lot of wild things about you.*"

Harlan blew her a kiss; she blew him one back, and he pulled away as she walked up the front steps to her house.

CHAPTER ELEVEN

Buddy didn't wait till Amanda arrived at the hospital. He left Darcy in Cal's able hands and drove the three-quarters of a mile over to the Stone residence. It was a two-story brick house with floor-to-ceiling French windows and a paved driveway that wove around oak trees to the front door. It sat dead center on four acres of shaded ground and velvet grass. Harlan had not adhered to his father's teachings on living below his means. His mother had encouraged him to build in the new Bel-Manor section of town, and he had given Darcy full reins on designing and decorating their dream house.

Two police cars were in the driveway, and one officer was standing in the backyard smoking. Buddy got out of his city-issued Chevrolet and looked at the youthful patrolman like an officer of the day would look at a private and said, "You know how to field strip that thing, soldier?"

"Yes sir."

"Then be sure you do it in case the chief should pull up."

"He's not coming, is he?"

"I seriously doubt it," Buddy said as he smiled at the young policeman. "Anything look strange here?"

"Not to my eye. I never touched anything. It's just like they left it. You're the first person been here since they took the two of them to the hospital."

Buddy looked around the backyard. He could see the pool and the grape arbor and the two-car garage from where he stood. He walked to the back porch and looked in before stepping inside. It was his police training, even though he knew there was no danger lying ahead. He opened the door, then walked through the screened porch area and into the kitchen and stopped. There was the chair from their dinette set lying on its side against the cabinets. It was the only thing out of place except for spilled salt and pepper shakers on the table. This must have happened when Harlan fell on the tabletop from the force of the bullet. Buddy walked back and jiggled the door handle and looked for any wood shavings that might have fallen when the door was pushed in.

"Have they dusted for prints in here?" he yelled out to the uniform in the yard.

"Yes sir."

Buddy walked slowly back to the open door and looked at the young, grinning, apparently rookie officer. "I thought you said nobody had been here."

"Oh, well, yeah. I meant nobody but those guys looking for evidence."

"What did they find?"

"Don't know. They were sweeping stuff up and brushing stuff on and taking pictures and I don't know what all. I never worked a shooting before. You?"

"Yeah."

"You ever shot anybody?"

"How long have you been a cop … what's your name?"

"Snyder. Jesse Snyder."

"How long you been a cop, Jesse?"

"'Bout two months. Why?"

Jesse's question went unanswered as Buddy wandered deeper into the house, carefully checking all windows and doors. He went into each room and looked for nothing in particular and everything in general. Darcy had said the man had not gone anywhere but the kitchen, but he searched each room with the question in his mind about why the man was there at all. And what was here that was worth introducing a gun into the matter? He walked through the upstairs rooms where the kids slept. He looked out the windows of the master bedroom just to see what could be seen of the driveway and anyone who might approach the house from that direction. He walked back down the steps slowly and listened to the silence of the house. As he walked through the dining room, near the kitchen, he could still smell the lingering odor of gunpowder. He stood in the kitchen and replayed everything Darcy had told him in his mind until he could see, with his eyes closed, the scene as it happened. He could feel it and hear it, and his senses were on edge with the fear he knew they both had experienced.

After nearly twenty minutes, he closed the kitchen door behind him, then the back porch door, and walked toward his unmarked Chevy.

"Why?" Jesse Snyder asked again.

"What?"

"Why do you want to know how long I been a cop?"

"Oh, I was just thinking it was time I put you in for a promotion."

"Really?" Jesse stood swollen with expectant glory as Buddy got in his car, shook his head at nobody in particular, and drove off.

CHAPTER TWELVE

"Poppa, don't you want me to bring you something to eat?"

"Nah. I'm not hungry."

"You never eat lunch. And you should let me bring you something."

"You're sounding like your mother now. If I was hungry, I'd eat. But I'm not. And you'll see, boy. The older you get the less you need to eat. You'll see. Ain't that right, Fritz?"

Fritz just smiled his yellow smile and shook his head. He was a small, one-hundred-and-forty-pound man who stood, at best, five feet six inches tall in his bedroom shoes. And that's all anyone who knew him had ever seen him wear: leather, backless bedroom shoes with dress socks and gabardine pants. He wore white but yellowing and frayed dress shirts and one of an assortment of three ties. On most days, he wore a vest, but on all days he wore his glasses with the attached jewelers' glass and a green visor. He looked like a mob bookkeeper from a Warner Brothers gangster movie. And he smelled of cigarette smoke and chicken broth regardless of the time of day. He spoke, when he spoke, with an indistinguishable accent. Harlan never liked him and communicated with him as infrequently as possible. He passed notes to him for the work he needed done, and few if any words were exchanged between them in a day's time. The only person who ever talked to Fritz was H. V., and since his illness, he would sit for hours with Fritz every day.

Harlan had asked his father about Fritz many times. Even as a boy he had questions that were never answered clearly.

"Poppa. Who is Fritz?"

"What do you mean who is he? He's my employee and the best jeweler on the East Coast."

"Where did he come from?"

"Came from the old country."

"What old country?"

"Don't be disrespectful, boy. He's your elder. Don't let me catch you making fun of him."

"I'm not making fun of him, Poppa. He just kinda scares me. He never says much—just grunts. And he smells funny."

"Don't you worry about old Fritz. He's all right. Loyal to a T."

"Where does he live?"

"'Cross town. Why are you so curious about old Fritz?"

"I don't know. I don't think he likes me."

"He likes you, son. Just don't bother him. He's busy."

And that was all Harlan or any of the family or townspeople knew about the little man who had occupied the back room of Stone's for the past twenty years.

But Fritz's identity and value had been the last things on Harlan's mind these past three weeks. The mystery that was haunting him most nights and practically all of the days was, "Who is Darcy

Brennaman?" She had not given him her phone number, and even though he had looked it up in the telephone directory, assuming her daddy was Howard Brennaman on Route 3 in Harrison Springs, he hadn't called for all the right reasons. If she had truly wanted him to call, she would have given it to him when he asked for it. He wasn't used to this sort of behavior. Most girls gave him their phone numbers and addresses and places of work without him even asking. This one was playing hard to get. Or maybe she just wasn't interested. He wasn't used to that, either.

He had originally thought she would call him at the store within the next day or so, but when that didn't happen, he was bewildered. He tried to relive their conversation in the car to see if he had offended her, but he could think of nothing that would have left her this cold. And then there was the kiss she blew him just before he pulled off. She wouldn't have done that if she didn't have some interest in seeing him again. He spent his days between customers and bookkeeping trying to come up with the right approach to instigate their next meeting. So far he had no ideas. Maybe he'd just drive out there and knock on the door. But that would leave him vulnerable to her rejecting him completely. He had never faced such a situation with a girl before. He couldn't get the memory of her out of his mind nor her face out of his dreams.

It was a late Sunday afternoon, and the sunshine and heat of a perfect summer day was beginning to turn black. Harlan and his date had been at the lake most of the day. He dropped her off at her house and promised to call the next day, but in his mind he was fairly sure he wouldn't. She was pretty in a small-town sort of way and looked inviting in her swimsuit, but after an hour with her on the manmade beach of Lake Shenandoah, he was lost for any conversation. He tried *to show interest but finally just gave up and soaked up the sun, took a few dips, and then took her home. He wasn't even sure she believed that he would call the next day. And maybe she didn't even want him to. He really didn't care. His mind and his heart weren't it. And if it hadn't been for that first powerful clap of thunder that brought him out of his reverie, he might have ridden right by the girl and dog. But somewhere in the seconds between the thunder burst and the next flash of lightning, the rain poured as suddenly as if there were a giant hole in the cloud overhead. That's when he saw the girl and the golden retriever walking on the right-hand side of the road. They were drenched before he could hit his brakes. They began running, but there was no shelter in sight. He blew his car horn, pulled up beside them, rolled down the window, and said, "Get in quick, or you both are going to drown."*

They didn't resist. The dog jumped in first, and his mistress followed as if he had her on a leash instead of the other way around. It wasn't until she closed the door and wiped her hair from her eyes that he saw it was the girl from his dreams. They recognized each other at the same moment and broke into a laughing fit. The old dog started barking, and Harlan and Darcy laughed even harder.

"What are you doing out here in the rain?"

"Well, it wasn't raining when we started walking. I could see it coming, but we were too far away from the house to get there. So here we are."

"Where are you going?"

"We were just walking. This is Sam. He's my aunt's dog. We're visiting her this afternoon, and I thought I'd take him for a walk."

Sam barked again at the mention of his name, and Harlan rubbed his smelly wet head.

"Sam, this is the second time in three weeks that I've rescued this girl, and she won't give me the time of day. What do you suggest I do to get her attention?"

Sam barked again and tried to lick his face.

Pulling her hair back, Darcy said, *"If I didn't know better, I would think you were following me."*

"How do you know better? Maybe I am. Why haven't you called me?"

Harlan pulled away from the curb, not knowing where he was going but just glad to have her in the car with him. She finally said, *"Take a left right down here. My aunt lives in that second house on the left."*

When he stopped in the driveway, Darcy opened the door and let Sam out; he dashed through the rain, heading for the comfort and shelter of his front porch. She closed the car door quickly to keep any more rain from soaking the seats and then turned and looked at Harlan.

"Thanks again. You always show up in the nick of time. I mean what are the odds that you, of all people, would come along just at that moment?"

"You haven't answered my question. Why haven't you called me?"

Darcy sat for a long time and looked out the windshield as if she were trying to find the right words in the rain. Finally she turned and looked at him, and with a serious and solemn tone to her voice said, *"I'm afraid of you, Harlan Stone. You scare me."*

"You're all wrong. I'm the one who's scared. I'm scared I'll never see you again."

Harlan was used to making all the right moves, but this time he was the one caught off guard. Darcy, with the bright eyes and sweet face, *leaned toward him and kissed him softly. Her lips were cool and still wet. When she pulled back, she sat for just a moment.*

The rain on the roof of the car was the only sound for what seemed liked minutes. But it was really only seconds before she said, "I'll give you my phone number when you pick me up at seven thirty tomorrow evening."

And then she was gone.

Chapter Thirteen

Six forty-five, and the morning shift was starting to gather in all areas of the hospital. It was like a waking-up process. Nurses and staff were coming in all the doors, and lighthearted early-morning conversations filled what had been the silent air of the waiting room. Somewhere a radio played in the background. Johnny Horton was singing "The Battle of New Orleans." Car horns and singing birds were heard each time the automatic door opened to let in another freshly dressed member of the medical profession. The nurses walked in pairs and talked while the doctors walked alone with their heads down to avoid being detained or buttonholed by an anxious patient. And the essential coffee aroma mercifully permeated and overrode the distasteful yet always present medicinal fetor. Another day at Lenity General had begun. Before the day was over, lives would be saved, sicknesses would be healed, failures would be met—and then tomorrow it would start all over again with the same sights, sounds, and smells.

"Coffee smells good. You want some more?" Cal asked.

Darcy shook her head.

"You want me to find you a newspaper or magazine?"

"No."

"Then talk to me. Don't just sit there with your thoughts. Get it out."

She smiled and squeezed Cal's hand. "You're his oldest friend in the world. You know him better than probably even me."

"I've known him longer. But I don't know about better."

"Sure you do. You two guys—or I should say, you three guys—have secrets and memories no one else will ever know about."

"We have a few miles behind us."

"Cal, what if he doesn't live?"

"He'll live."

"Will you go in the hospital chapel and pray for him?"

"I don't have to go anywhere. I've been praying for him sitting right here. But if you would feel better, we can go there."

"No. I don't want to go. I'm afraid they won't know where to find me if they need me. And I really don't want you to leave. I guess I'm not making much sense, am I?"

"You're doing fine."

"I keep seeing the look on his face when he fell back against that table. I just knew he was dead. I must have screamed louder then than when I first saw that man in our kitchen. Have you ever been afraid like that—to where your mind just froze?"

"Sure. For about four years in the war. I was that scared every day. So was everybody else. The ones who aren't scared are crazy."

"What were you scared of? Dying?"

"That and worse."

"What's worse than dying?"

"Living. Suffering. Loss. Dying is not that hard when it's time. But you need to get that out of your mind for now."

"Have you talked to Ellie lately?"

"Oh, yeah. We talk about every other day."

"She okay? Do you think she'll ever come to Mt. Jefferson?"

"That's two questions and two different answers."

Darcy laughed. "I do that a lot, don't I? Ask two questions at one time."

"Yes, you do. And Harlan has noticed it, too. He thinks it's funny. But to answer your dual questions—yes, she's okay, and no, I don't think she'll ever come to Mt. Jefferson."

"Do you still love her?"

"I'm supposed to be comforting you, and here you are ministering to me. How did the tables get turned around here, girl?"

They both laughed, and Cal could see a little color coming back to her cheeks and a hint of the warmth back in her eyes.

"Yes, I still love her," Cal answered honestly.

A nurse from the back came toward them, and they both froze until she walked past them to a vending machine. The automatic glass door opened again, and someone came in from outside.

"Amanda! I knew you'd come."

Darcy and Amanda stood and hugged long and hard and cried together like the old friends they were. Cal and Amanda made eye contact just as he and Buddy had less than an hour ago out of Darcy's sight. She winked, and he smiled and felt that things would be better now.

Chapter Fourteen

According to Harlan, things went much too slow; according to Darcy, much too fast. They fought one another on the tempo of the relationship, but in doing so, found their rhythm as a couple. Harlan would have married her within two weeks if she had only given him half a sign. He confessed to her that his wild oats were behind him and that she was the perfect wife he had been looking for all his adult life. She accepted this compliment with the grace of the modern girl she was but held him at arm's length until she was sure he was as much in love with her as she was with him. And she wasn't the only person Harlan had to convince. Her father had his concerns also.

Darcy and her father sat on the front-porch steps of the beautiful old farmhouse one early fall evening; she with a sweater thrown over her shoulders and he in his bib overalls and work shoes.

"Tell me about your man, Darcy."

"Not much to tell you don't already know. He's the prettiest man I've ever seen, and I think I love him."

"Pretty? That's a peculiar way of describing a man."

They both laughed. Howard Brennaman's smile faded first, and he looked off and squinted into the sunset and said, "Have you met his old daddy yet? H. V."

"Yeah. We had supper with them a couple of weeks ago. They're both real nice. She's kind of quiet but just a real sweet lady. He's a little ... what can I say ... more outgoing, maybe?"

"What do you know about him?"

"Who? Harlan or his dad?"

"The old man. What does Harlan say about him?"

It was Darcy's turn to look into the sunset and reflect a moment before answering.

"It's hard to say. He doesn't talk about him much. He talks more about his mother. And when they're all together, they sort of talk through Mrs. Stone. But not to each other. You know what I mean?"

"Darcy ... " he began, then paused.

"What? What's wrong?"

He looked at her flush in the eyes, not father to daughter, but adult to adult.

"Darcy, you know that Stone is not their last name, don't you?"

"What are you talking about? Of course it's Stone."

Howard rubbed his rough, callused hands and struggled for the right words.

"Stone is the name the old man took on when he moved here years ago and started the diamond and watch business. His real name is Stonebrunner."

"German?"

"Actually, Jewish.

There was a cold silence on the steps of the Brennaman farm as the sun sank a little deeper behind the trees and the temperature dropped a couple of degrees. Darcy waited for her father to continue, and he waited for her to reply. And after an interlude of quiet tension between the two of them, Darcy studied the worried look on her daddy's weathered face and asked, "How do you know that?"

"A lot of people know that, honey."

"Well, it certainly is no sin to be Jewish." Her tone was defiant and protective.

"Never said there was. I'm just telling you something I thought you might not know."

"What if he is Jewish? What does it matter?" There was a sound of tears in her voice.

"It doesn't matter to him at all, I'm sure. But I just want to know if it matters to you."

"Of course it doesn't. I don't look down my nose at anybody."

"Darcy, it's not a case of looking down your nose. Now don't get all riled up and make something more out of this than needs to be."

"You're the one that brought it up, Daddy."

"Yes. Yes, I am. And I didn't bring it up to put them down. It's just something I wanted to be sure you knew. Because, honey, it's a lot of difference for you and for them. It seems that you and Harlan are getting real close and maybe real serious. I'm not throwing a wrench in anything, but I just want you to be careful you don't get hurt."

"How would I get hurt?"

"They might be the ones who throw the wrench in things. Be careful, sweetie. Harlan may not be as serious as you are, and his parents may not approve of you as much as you think they do."

"They seem to like me just fine, and I like them."

"But ... that's as Harlan's girlfriend. When they see you might become Harlan's wife someday, things might be different."

"Just what are you saying, Daddy? Do you not approve of them, or do you think they won't approve of us?"

"Darcy, being Jewish is two things. A race and a religion. I got no problem with the race. But when you start mixing up their beliefs with our Presbyterian beliefs, life can get complicated. Children get involved, and somebody has to say that Jesus ain't all that important in order to make the marriage work. Do you hear what I'm saying?"

"Do you think I'd renounce my beliefs?"

"I think you might be asked to. And you might find it sort of difficult for two people to live under the same roof with those kinds of differences."

"Not Harlan and me, Daddy. We can handle it."

"Love can only do so much, little girl. Don't overestimate it."

"And don't you worry about me. I'm not going away from my beliefs. You can count on that. And here's something else, Daddy. His best friend, Cal Vaxter, is in seminary school to be a Methodist preacher. So you see, their religion has never been a problem. They're as close as David and Jonathan."

Howard had to laugh at this. But then, with a smile on his face, he made his final point.

"He and this Vaxter boy never had any kids together, did they?"

Darcy slapped her father playfully on the arm and said, *"Don't worry. All of my children will be raised as little Presbyterians."*

He looked at his beautiful daughter long and hard. She always made him smile.

"I notice you've never brought Harlan to church with you, honey."

"No. But I will. And then you'll see."

CHAPTER FIFTEEN

Mt. Jefferson, with a population of twenty-two thousand in the last national census before 1959, was too small of a town for many people who drove through it on Route 250, east to west, or Route 11, north to south. It didn't have everything an out-of-towner might be looking for, but it had everything its citizens needed. There was a pretty nice old hotel on the hill overlooking the east end of town with a large neon sign announcing its unusual name: Lee-Jackson Hotel. It had been an elegant place for travelers to rest and dine around the turn of the century, but fifty-nine more years had taken a toll. It was in need of some mortar work, some fresh paint, and some letters in the sign that made you think twice about checking into the Lee- ackson otel. It still boasted a wonderful restaurant in the former ballroom that was packed by after-church lunch-goers every Sunday. The old hotel looked down on eight blocks of small town life that looked like a Norman Rockwell painting.

On the right side of the street was the Crown Theater with its marquee full of first-run movies, and around the corner was the

Strand, with its marquee full of double features, B movies, and serials. On that same block were dress shops for women of all walks of life: Kindleberg's and Lilly Mae's for the finest in evening and Sunday wear for the upper class, then the less expensive versions of the same things at the Dress Shop and Margo's just doors down. Montgomery Ward and Benson's Department Store were on up the street a couple of blocks, and in between were a number of five-and-dime stores such as Newberry's and McCroy's and Macalbee's.

There was a hardware store called Vaxter Brothers on the corner of Central and Main, and every Saturday morning from about eight till noon, farmers and husbands and loafers in general, many who were in town while their wives shopped, would gather in front of Vaxter's and stand and talk and smoke and tell jokes and lies. It was a human traffic jam on the sidewalk there every week no matter how hot or cold or dry or wet the weather might get. Paul and Ernest, the Vaxter brothers, could be seen out among the crowd with their coffee cups in their hands, encouraging the gathering that would eventually spill inside and turn into an abundance of sales. By noon the wives had finished shopping and would come by and one by one take their talk-weary hubbies home.

There was a Blue Checker grocery store on the far end of the westernmost block downtown. Scattered throughout the other blocks were a few men's clothing stores—Matthew's, the Suit Closet, and one simply called the Men's Store. Dartmouth's Drugstore was on one side of Main while Clark's Drug and Fountain was on the other. Both offered over-the-counter remedies, prescriptions by local and friendly pharmacists, a cosmetics section, and a lunch counter serving sandwiches and ice cream in little pointed paper cups that sat in chrome holders. But if you required a little more of your dining experience and didn't want to wait till the weekend for the buffet room at the Lee- ackson otel, then there was Drakos or Mulligans.

Most of the people in Mt. Jefferson didn't know where Nick Drakos came from. Some didn't care, some didn't ask, and some didn't want the responsibility of knowing. But for those few who took the time to find out, they knew he first set foot on American soil on July 6, 1914. He and his little brother and his parents were on one of the last steamships from Greece that landed at Locust Point on the coast of Baltimore. They had sailed the Mediterranean and then the Atlantic from Port Pylos, southwest of Athens, when Nick was only eleven years old. Arriving in the Baltimore harbor just days before that port was closed due to World War I, the Drakos family was met by an older cousin who had sent for them to come join the community and the family business. But the look on the cousin's face when he met them told another story. The business was no longer, and there was no place for the new arrivals to live.

After changing their drachmas to American dollars, the family continued south in the United States by bus. Their goal was Atlanta, where an uncle had two large restaurants and a promise of employment and housing. But the money ran out en route, and they found themselves in a little southern town called Mt. Jefferson. The first two weeks, they slept in the city park until Nick's father could make enough money shining shoes, tending gardens, and cleaning floors to get them proper shelter. Within three years, they had their own business on the corner of Main Street; their mamma did the cooking and their father served as manager and host, and Nick and his brother waited tables and washed dishes. From the summer

of 1917, this location was home to a restaurant with the name of
Drakos above the door.

The restaurant began as little more than a counter and a couple
of tables. After his father's death, Nick took over and bought the
store next door, which housed a spool and yarn shop. The dividing
wall came down, and that was when the round tables and white
tablecloths were added and the counter was removed. Nick had
grown up, and Drakos had grown with him.

Everyone who walked in the front door was greeted by one of
two sights. Either Nick himself coming toward them with open arms,
a cigarette firmly between his lips, or his beautiful wife, Christina,
smiling and reaching for their hands while Nick sat at the last table
next to the kitchen, smoking and reading the racing forms. Either
way, customers were made to feel at home and left with the sense that
the Drakos family wanted them back. There was even a small verse
printed on the bottom of each menu:

All are welcome, all are fed

Give us Lord, our daily bread

Nick Drakos was everyone's friend. His wife was gorgeous, his
sons were handsome, and his daughter, with black shining eyes and
black shining hair, was angelic. Nick was fond of saying, "No one
leaves Drakos without feeling loved."

The other restaurant of note was Mulligans. But that's a story
yet to be told.

CAL VAXTER

CHAPTER SIXTEEN

Cal sat with the two women while Darcy told him and Amanda the story of how she and Harlan had come into their kitchen and discovered the stranger standing in the middle of the floor.

"He was just there all of a sudden. And he was kind of hunched over."

"What do you mean 'hunched over'?" Amanda asked.

"I don't know. It was kind of funny looking. And he had this clown face on."

"A painted face?"

"No. One of those plastic masks with the string in the back. But it looked like a clown. It had a red nose and big round eyes."

"Did he say anything?" Cal asked.

"Yeah, he said something, but I'm not sure what. It wasn't real clear. But that's when Harlan got really mad and threw a dinette chair at him."

"Did he hit him?" Amanda's eyes were full of concern.

"He might have. The guy sort of ducked, but it might have hit him. I'm not sure. But then that's when I first saw the gun. Then I heard the shot and saw Harlan fall."

"What did the man do when Harlan fell? Did he come toward him or run?" Cal surprised himself with this question and thought he sounded more like Buddy than the family minister.

"I ran toward Harlan, and I can honestly say I didn't really see the man run out the door. He must have, but all my attention was on Harlan at the time, and I didn't see him."

"Weren't you afraid he might shoot again?" Amanda asked.

"I wasn't thinking clear enough to reason anything like that. I just made a lunge toward Harlan. I grabbed him to keep him from hitting the floor. It was all so fast, it was really just a blur. And thinking back on it, it already seems like a dream. A dream that happened days or weeks ago."

"You don't have to talk anymore about it to us, honey. Cal and I understand, and you can just sit here and rest. You don't have to say a word."

"But I feel like I need to talk about it. And then when I do, I don't want to. It's the most mixed-up feelings I've ever had in my life."

"That's all right. That's all right."

Amanda put her arm around her friend, and Cal patted her shoulder before he got up and walked back toward the nurses' station. He checked his watch against the wall clock—7:31 a.m.—and started to ask the RN behind the counter if she could find out how the surgery was going, but he knew this was an amateurish question. She wouldn't know and wouldn't tell him if she did. So he decided instead to use the phone across the hall, where he could still keep his eye on any doctor or nurse that might approach Darcy. He wanted to be with her when any news came.

He pulled the folding glass door to the booth open and sat down inside. Then he dropped his dime in the slot and gave the operator all the necessary long-distance information. The phone on the other end rang four times before someone answered.

"Hello."

"Ellie? Sorry to call so early."

"That's okay. What's wrong?"

"Some bad news on this end. Harlan's in the hospital."

"What happened?"

"Somebody shot him. And I either just wanted to let you know or I needed to talk to you. For the life of me, I don't know which."

CHAPTER SEVENTEEN

If handsome *was the one word that described Harlan Stone, then* rugged *was the single word that summarized Cal Vaxter. He was always a little taller than Harlan, a little thinner, and his good looks were only obvious after you were around him awhile. Boys in his era tended to get their hair cut short only for the summer; Cal wore his that way year-round. He was gangly even at ten years old and didn't fill out until his midteens. Neither he nor Harlan could remember a time they weren't best friends. Their very earliest of memories included one another, even though their families were anything but close. H. V. Stone and Ernest Vaxter had stores three doors away from one another for over twenty years, but the only regular greetings they ever exchanged were a few words at the quarterly downtown merchants meetings or a hand wave as one passed the other's storefront. The boys' mothers spoke on the phone occasionally, but only to inquire if one boy was at the other's house and, if so, to tell him to come home for supper.*

Main Street and all the alleys of the side streets in Mt. Jefferson were home to Little Cal, as he was known all over the town by every store owner, clerk, and salesperson. His parents, Ernest and Loretta, and his aunt Betty Bell and uncle Paul were the proprietors of the only hardware store inside the city limits. From the time he could walk, he played under the desks in the back-room office and explored every cubbyhole in the basement and attic of Vaxter Brothers at 221 Main. As he got older, in his preschool days, he roamed the sidewalks, wandering in and out of all the neighboring stores, and was simultaneously the darling and the bane of every merchant on the block. Little Cal was both loved and feared by everyone who knew him, and as he grew into young manhood, he carried that same dual charm with all his peers, friend or foe.

Cal and Harlan were born only twenty-three days apart, so they experienced every aspect of life together. One was never ahead of the other, nor was one ever lagging far behind. But if one was ever pushing the other, it was Little Cal and his daring and sometimes dangerous ideas, even at the tender age of ten.

Early one Saturday morning, they were in the aisle of Vaxter Brothers, tossing fistfuls of ten-penny nails into a bin to see who could get the most points from twelve feet away.

"What time does the movie start?" Harlan asked.

"Ten o'clock. You know that. It always starts at ten o'clock."

"A couple of weeks ago it didn't start till eleven."

"That was because the projector broke down, stupid. It's always ten o'clock on Saturdays," Cal assured him.

"You know what's playing this morning?"

"It don't matter. We're going anyway, ain't we?"

"Yeah, I guess. But let's walk down there and see what it is. 'Cause if it's a love picture, I ain't going."

"It won't be no love picture. Not on a Saturday morning. Matter of fact, I think it will be Tom Mix. I think that's what the previews said last week."

"How much money you got?" Harlan asked, stopping to count what was in his pocket.

"I got enough, but we ain't going to need any this morning."

"Why won't we?" Harlan asked as he tossed his last nail, watching it bounce out of the bin and into the hardwood floor.

"I got an idea. I was walking by the Crown the other day, and I noticed ..."

"What in heaven's name are you two doing now?" It was Cal's uncle Paul. *"Quit throwing those ten-penny nails. Just look at the holes you've made in the floor. Now both of you get on out of here. And don't come back till you're at least twenty-five."*

Cal and Harlan hurried out the door while Cal's uncle was still mumbling about the damage they had caused and ran a half a block before they quit laughing and slowed to a walking pace.

"What's your idea?" Harlan asked.

"I was walking by the Crown the other day, and I noticed the two doors. The one on the right of the box office is the door you go in, right?"

"Right."

"The one on the left is the door you come out."

"Right again."

"So I figure if we wait till everyone pays and goes in, Mr. Hardy always leaves the box office and goes to help out at the popcorn stand. So all we have to do is wait till he leaves, and we go in the coming-out door."

"Why?" Harlan asked in all sincerity.

"We get in free, stupid."

"Why? Don't you have enough money to pay?"

*"That's not the point, Harlan. The point is we get in free. We sneak
in the other door. 'Course there's only one problem."*

"What's that?"

*"We'll have to walk in backwards. That way if we get caught, we can
say we were leaving. See what I mean?"*

"I don't know. What if we do get caught?"

*"First off, we won't. Second off, if we do, we'll tell them we were just
leaving."*

"And third off?" Harlan challenged him.

"Third off, we run like a striped monkey."

This doubled them over in a fit of laughter that caused other
pedestrians on the street to turn and stare. Pretty soon everyone who
saw them was laughing also, only they didn't know why. They were just
laughing at two young boys on a bright spring Saturday morning who
were having the time of their lives.

It was Tom Mix. And his Wonder Horse, Tony. And the name of the
movie was The Great K & A Train Robbery. And Mr. Hardy did leave
the box office as soon as every kid was off the sidewalk and in the theater.
And Little Cal Vaxter and Harlan Stone did walk in the exit door
backward. And some nineteen-year-old college boy in a maroon usher
suit and a black bow tie did grab them by the collars and escort them
back out the same exit door. And they both did stand in the morning
sunlight on East Main Street and laugh till tears ran down their cheeks.
And then they stood at the box office window until Mrs. Hardy saw them
waiting, and they each gave her the nine-cents admission price, took a
gray ticket, and entered the world of charm and adventure the way they
were supposed to. And the way Tom Mix meant them to.

CHAPTER EIGHTEEN

"Cal, just tell me what happened. It's after seven thirty, and I don't have a lot of time."

"That's it. Somebody shot him. And I'm already sorry I called. I know you're getting ready to go to work. Just let it go, and I'll talk to you tonight or tomorrow."

"You most certainly will not. You don't just call and tell me your best friend has been shot and then leave me hanging. You called to tell me about it, so go ahead and tell me."

"I don't know much more than that."

"Well, who did it?"

"We don't know."

"Where did it happen?"

"At their house."

"Is he dead?"

"Is he dead? You're so tactful, Ellie. And you have such warmth in your voice. Look, I'm sorry I called. Just let it go."

"No, tell me. Is he?"

"He's not dead, Ellie. He's in surgery right now, and I'm sitting here with Darcy and Amanda. We're waiting for some kind of word as soon as the doctor comes out."

"Let me talk to Darcy."

"She's not close. She's down the hall. How are the kids?"

"They're fine."

"Are either one of them nearby? I'll talk to whichever one is there."

"They're both here. It's seven thirty in the morning, Cal. Where would you think they would be?"

"I meant are they there in the room …"

"No, they're not. Matthew's in the bathroom, and Elizabeth is dressing. You can call them tonight if you want to talk to them. Matthew has to be at summer school in thirty minutes, and Elizabeth has to be at work at eight thirty. And look at the time. I'm going to be late for work myself. I suppose Elizabeth told you she got a summer job babysitting for the Hinkels down the street."

"Yes, she told me."

"Okay then. If you don't have any more information, I've got to go."

"Tell them I'll talk to them tonight."

"Don't call too early this evening. We're all supposed to go on an office picnic, and we may not be home till dark."

"Look, I'll just wait and call sometime tomorrow."

"Well, tomorrow is Saturday, and I can't be sure we'll be here. We may go over to Louisville to Mother and Dad's. Mother's been wanting us to come and spend the weekend."

"That's fine. I'll talk to you and them whenever I can find you."

"And, Cal, don't call too often. Because every time you do, it just gets them both upset."

"Gets you upset too, doesn't it, Ellie? Only in a different way."

"I don't have time to argue with you this morning. So let's just leave it at that. I'm sorry about your friend, but there's nothing I can do. Good-bye."

Cal didn't even attempt to say good-bye. The dial tone was buzzing in his ear as he sat there in the stuffy phone booth, looking down the hallway of the hospital. Near the end he could see Darcy and Amanda still sitting, talking, and waiting. Many thoughts crossed his mind, but the one that lingered was that he wished it were him instead of Harlan lying back there with his life in the balance. He knew if that were the case, his prayers would be a lot different than they had been this morning.

Chapter Nineteen

Little Cal and Harlan roamed the streets most of the summer days that they weren't home riding their bikes around the neighborhood, to and from the public swimming pool. Cal loved to go into Macalbee's Five and Dime to get a bag of hot popcorn to carry around as they wove in and out of the stores, killing time and finding trouble to get into and out of. Harlan continuously found himself embroiled in whatever scheme Cal could think up on the spot.

"Here's what we'll do," Cal said one afternoon. "I picked up an empty paper sack from behind the counter at my dad's store. I've got it in my pocket."

"So?" Harlan asked, not sure what new plan was growing in his friend's devious mind.

"We'll go in Macalbee's, and we'll each get a bag of popcorn. It's really good stuff. And as soon as we pay for it, we'll go out the front door and around the corner."

"Why?"

"Just follow me, and I'll show you."

They did just that, and Tildy, the little woman who operated the lunch counter, went to the popcorn machine and dipped them each a five-cent bag of buttery popcorn, filled and overflowing. They paid and politely said, "Thank you," and then turned and quickly went out the front door and around the corner. Cal stopped short and immediately pulled the paper sack from his hip pocket and poured all but a few kernels of corn into it. He handed it to Harlan and said, "You stay here, and I'll be right back." Then he left his cohort standing on the street, out of sight of Tildy, with two bags of popcorn: one in a Macalbee's bag and one in a Vaxter Brothers bag.

With tears in his eyes, Little Cal burst through the doors of the dime store and went straight to Tildy, who was wiping down the counter.

"I dropped my popcorn," he announced.

"Aw, honey. I am so sorry."

"It spilled all over the sidewalk, and I don't have any more money."

"Now don't you worry, sweetie. We'll get you another bag." She scooped a new bag, full to the brim again, and said as she handed it down to him, "You be careful now that you don't spill this one."

"I won't, ma'am. And thank you very much."

By the time he rounded the corner where Harlan was waiting, his tears had turned to a huge smile, and they had three bags of Macalbee's popcorn for the price of two.

Evidence that Cal and Harlan had accepted Buddy as a full-time partner in their exclusive little club—after that fateful day on the playground—came in the form of including him in some of their underhanded, if not criminal, scams. After discovering that the new kid, Buddy Briggs, lived just a few blocks away from them on Maple Street, it was now a trio that was spotted on bike trips and downtown excursions.

It was definitely all three eleven-year-olds who took part in the bottle caper after school one day.

"I've got an idea how to make some money."

"You're always coming up with crazy ideas, Cal. Is it safe and is it legal?" Buddy asked with a smile.

"You know it isn't if he's coming up with it." Harlan laughed.

"Listen, guys. This is a good one. A surefire one, and no one will ever catch on. And it's legal."

"Yeah, sure." Buddy and Harlan both laughed.

"Really. You know how stores will give you a penny for empty Coca-Cola bottles?"

"Yeah."

"Well, that isn't illegal, is it?"

"No, I guess not," Buddy said as he looked to Harlan for agreement. Harlan nodded.

"Okay. All we have to do is gather up some bottles and take them in and get the money for them."

"We could go along the highway and get some that people throw out of their cars or go over to the ballpark and find some under the bleachers." Buddy was getting excited about it.

"No. No. No. No. That's too much work. You know down the street from my daddy's hardware store where Mulligans Restaurant is? He'll give you a penny for any empty bottle just like grocery stores do because he sells Coca-Cola in there and they come every week to deliver them."

"Okay," Harlan said, "then we just have to gather a bunch of them up."

"No. That's where my idea comes in. Out behind his restaurant, in the alley, he stacks up all his empties for a week at a time. So all we have

to do is get a box and go back in the alley, fill up the box, and take them around front to the restaurant and get a penny a piece for them."

"But he'd be buying his own bottles," Harlan said, looking to Buddy for confirmation.

"Exactly," Cal assured them. "But we ain't doing nothing wrong. We're bringing empties in and getting paid for them. Nobody ever said where the empties have to come from. We can do this all week long."

"He'll catch on."

"We won't do it every day, stupid. We'll skip a day now and then."

"I don't know, Cal. We could get in a lot of trouble." Buddy was already feeling butterflies in his stomach.

"How? There's no way he could ever figure it out. It's surefire."

"Isn't he your uncle or something?" Harlan asked.

"Sort of."

"What do you mean, sort of?" Buddy wondered out loud.

"He's my aunt's brother. My aunt Betty Bell's brother. She's married to my uncle, and he's her brother. So he's just sort of my uncle. I call him that, but he really isn't."

"I don't know. What do you think, Buddy?"

"I don't know either."

"Aw, come on. Let's try it just once. Just one time to see what happens."

And as with all of Little Cal's mischievous wiles, he sold it to his friends as something that couldn't fail. He never really fooled them, but he always sold them, so the three of them headed off for unseen alleys and another untried adventure.

Cal was the first to speak as they each carried a box of soda bottles in the front door of Mulligans. "Good evening, ma'am. We've been gathering up bottles and was wondering if you could give us the deposit on them."

"I'm kind of busy right now, sonny, but if you'll stand over to the side till these customers pay, I'll take care of you in a minute."

The three boys stood silently while Mabel Talley wiped her hands on her apron and stepped behind the glass counter to the cash register. A man and woman stood and paid their check and exchanged good-byes with her as they exited the front door. Then Mabel turned her attention back to the boys.

"All right, boys, what do you have here?"

Harlan and Buddy stood silent while Little Cal did all the talking. "We've got empty soda pop bottles."

"How many do you have?"

"We each have ten."

"Ten? How did you all come up with the same number?"

"Well, when we got to ten, we just quit gathering them. We figured a dime apiece is all we'd do today. Now, tomorrow we may have more."

Mabel hit the no-sale button, and the drawer flew open. She counted out three dimes and handed one to each boy, who in return said, "Thank you," and sat their box on the floor and went out the front door. They waited until they rounded the corner before they started jumping and laughing, but just as they did, Cal bumped into an extremely tall gentleman in a plaid three-piece suit.

"Whoa there, boys. You're going to knock somebody down."

They all three looked up, but only one of them spoke.

"Sorry, Uncle Vic."

"That's okay, Little Cal. You boys be careful now."

As they slowed their pace and the giant of a man disappeared in the door they had just come out of, it was Little Cal who spoke again.

"That was my uncle Vic. Just keep walking and don't look back."

They all three did and didn't. But the riches in their pockets helped them overcome their fear, and pretty soon anyone on the street could hear them whooping and hollering and laughing from block to block. It had worked just like Cal had promised it would, and there was no telling how much money they could make before the year was over.

CHAPTER TWENTY

Buddy Briggs came in the side door and found Amanda, Darcy, and Cal sitting quietly in the waiting area. He had no more than sat down than the heavy double doors opened and a man in surgical whites, a mask hanging from his neck, walked out and came to stand in front of the four of them.

"Hello, I'm Dr. Yandell. Are you Mrs. Stone?"

Darcy acknowledged she was, and the doctor continued.

"We're through with the surgery. He came through it just fine. The bullet tore a bit of his side, but it hit no main arteries; just some nonvital tissue. He may feel some numbness for a few weeks, even a month or so, but it will gradually go away. He should have complete use of his limb in good time. And that's about it. You can see him in about ten minutes. You can come on back with me now if you like and wait for them to wheel him in from the recovery room."

He looked the other three over and said as Darcy began to get up, "One of you can come with her if you like."

Darcy answered him without looking to the other three, "That's okay. I'll be fine. I want to see him for a few minutes alone, and then all of you can come back."

Dr. Yandell and Darcy disappeared behind the double doors.

"Well, that's good news," Amanda said to no one in particular.

"Sure is. But I'm a little surprised she didn't want you to go back with her."

"You know Darcy. She doesn't always react the way you think she's going to. She's very private, and to be real honest, since I got here—and Cal will bear me out on this—I've done most of the talking. She's had very little to say other than just to tell us what happened."

"I'm dreading what's coming next."

"What do you mean?"

"It's going to be up to me to make her talk more about it. And Harlan, too, just as soon as he's able. Pretty soon I'm going to have to treat them both in a more businesslike manner than I really want to."

"Well, for heaven sakes, honey, don't get rough with them. Give them some time."

"I can't give them any more time. I have to talk to the both of them just as soon as I can before this thing gets any colder."

Cal had said nothing while Buddy and Amanda talked. But then he looked at his old friend and said with a thoughtful and worried countenance, "We both need to talk to him professionally. You've got your questions, and I've got mine. But I was just thinking maybe we should go back there and see him as our friend first. Might make it a little more bearable for him if we ease into it."

"You're probably right, but when I talk to him, I'll have to ask you to leave."

Cal smiled. "That's okay. When I talk to him I'll have to ask you to leave too."

Amanda broke the hint of tension with, "One of you is looking out for his life and the other one is looking out for his soul. I'd say Harlan Stone is in good hands. You two have taken better care of him all his life than he has. And I'd better shut up before I say too much. Thank God he's going to be okay, and that's all I need to say."

Cal laughed and put his arm around Amanda.

"Amanda, my love, you should have been a judge. You have such a knack for bringing the short, blunt truth to light."

She hugged him back and said, "Was that Ellie you went to call a while ago?"

"And on top of everything else," Cal said directly to Buddy, "she's psychic."

"No. Just common sense," Amanda replied. "Who else would you be calling at seven thirty in the morning? How is she? And the kids?"

"I don't know about the kids. She wouldn't let me talk to them. She seldom does. They call me, and I try to call them when I know she's not there. This morning ... well, this morning I had a weak moment. I shouldn't have called. But I thought—silly me—that with all that was happening, maybe we could actually talk. But she showed her usual amount of warmth toward me and toward Harlan. 'Is he dead?' That was as much interest as she could muster up."

"Don't be too hard on her. This can't be easy for her, either."

"Then she could put a stop to it."

"I know, Cal. I know," Amanda said as she patted his arm.

"Hey, Reverend. If you're through pawing my wife and crying on her shoulder, let's go back there and be ready to see him as soon as we can."

"Leave your wife out of this, Lieutenant. And don't forget, I can still take you."

And just like in the old days, two friends, shoulder to shoulder, went through the double doors looking out for the third one.

CHAPTER TWENTY-ONE

Victor Albert Princeton, known to Little Cal and eventually to Harlan and Buddy as Uncle Vic, was the local celebrity of Mt. Jefferson. There had been a few others. There was an actor who called the town his birthplace but had left before the age of ten to subsequently find a certain amount of glory on the legitimate stage. He had costarred in a few Broadway plays and many road productions, a couple of which had played in the Crown on its way down the eastern coastal states. His name of fame meant little to the citizenry of Mt. Jefferson, as the name they saw in larger-than-life size on the marquee was Daniel King. Those who remembered him only had a few reminiscences of Danny Brusenbecker, who had danced and sung, "There's A Little Star Shining For You" in a grade school talent revue.

Mary McCabe Powers left her mark on the city library. She was born just doors away from it and wound up with her name attached to it for a time. After moving to New York as a young woman, she wrote a series of adventure books for girls, first published in 1901, that was recommended reading for third and fourth graders throughout the United States. She came back to visit once—when they christened the library the Mary McCabe Powers Library—but didn't stay long. Someone discovered that the man, twenty years her junior, who was traveling with her as her manager, was really her secret lover. After the ceremonies on a Friday evening, she was asked to leave and was gone before the sun rose on Saturday. Each year for nearly a decade there was an effort to get the city council to change the name back to the Mt. Jefferson Library, and after nine attempts by a number of determined committees, the proclamation was finally granted. But even years later, overdue books with Mary M. Powers Library stamped on their first blank pages would still pop up in boxes at auctions and flea markets.

But the real celebrity was Uncle Vic.

Vic Princeton was born before the turn of the century in a small apartment above his father's cigar store at 271 Culbertson Avenue. He went through the local school system and graduated with no particular honors and little fanfare. His popularity did not become evident until he moved to the Harrisburg, Pennsylvania, area a couple of years after completing his education. He found himself cleaning lockers and mowing the golf course at the Blue Ridge Country Club in the capital city. This opened the door for him to pick up jobs caddying for most of the local players and some of the pros who stopped in occasionally to play the links. The six-foot-five blond-haired teenager studied every swing and putt and absorbed every good and bad habit of every duffer and hustler he encountered. With a little help from the club pro, he found himself getting matches with some of the better players and then getting entered in a few amateur tournaments. Within eighteen months, he was being called a prodigy by the old timers. And before his twentieth birthday, he saw action in his first all-professional tournament that brought him *statewide recognition. A few more wins up the East Coast put him in the national spotlight, and pretty soon his trademark plaid knickers, pince- nez glasses, and precise putts on the green made him a permanent force in the world of sports.*

In the 1920s, he found his path to worldwide fame when he won the U.S. Open, the British Open, and two PGA Championships. The name Vic Princeton was on the lips of every sportscaster on three continents. He was in the newsreels in all the theaters. He was photographed giving lessons to Hollywood's most beautiful starlets. And there was a famous picture, one that made all the news services, of Calvin Coolidge and him teeing off side by side—both with big smiles and the little trademark glasses.

Vic never really left Mt. Jefferson. It was always a winter home for him to come back to, world-weary from his travels, and the hometown people loved having him among them. He brought a quiet and respectable air to the town and eventually established a business that would forever connect him to his roots. At the height of his popularity, he opened a restaurant on Main Street and named it Mulligans. The townspeople returned his favor by supporting him and making his celebrated little eatery a long-standing success. Many golf fans drove out of their way from all over America to eat lunch or dinner there. They came to try the Fairway Steak and the Greenside Salad and to see the pictures on the wall. Black-and-white pictures of Vic and Max Baer arm wrestling; one of Vic and the Babe each swinging a nine iron like a baseball bat; and even a picture of the four Marx Brothers deluging Vic with golf balls while he covered his head with his hands to protect himself.

Years before the public ever thought about it, Vic Princeton knew Mt. Jefferson was where he would retire. When the traveling got old and wore on his body and his nerves, this restaurant would be his shrine and his throne. He would have all he ever wanted and would never have to leave home again. His public would come to him—and they did for years and decades, just to get an autograph, a steak sandwich, and a handshake.

The little hellion who wreaked havoc up and down Main Street all of his adolescent life was no kin to Victor Princeton. Little Cal Vaxter called him Uncle Vic because he was the bachelor brother to Cal's aunt Betty Bell, who was the wife of Cal's uncle Paul, who was the brother of Cal's father, Ernest. Cal called men all over Mt. Jefferson uncle and referred to their wives by their first names, putting Miss in front of it.

This showed no disrespect but rather the proper respect. So when Little Cal's best friends started to call the world-famous Victor Princeton Uncle Vic, no one thought a thing about it. And how the feelings between them turned from fear and annoyance to love and respect was a story deeply imbedded in their early history.

CHAPTER TWENTY-TWO

Opening the cash register for change and moving boxes of empty soda bottles to the back became a standard three-day-a-week event. Every time the no-sale button caused the bell to chime as the drawer flew open, Vic looked up from his newspaper or bowl of soup or conversation he may have been having. And every time he did, he noticed the same three boys always standing at the exit counter with their hands out. One Friday afternoon, as the boys went out the door and joyfully past the front window, he watched them as they ran across the street, laughing and talking and punching one another. With his back to her as he still surveyed the street outside, Vic said, "Mabel. Those three boys. They're in here a lot?"

"Oh, yes. Two or three times a week."

"And always for the same thing." It was a statement more than a question.

"Always. Soda-pop bottles. I take them out back and put them with the others."

"How much do they usually collect?"

"Oh, usually fifteen cents or thirty cents. Something like that."

"Fifteen or thirty. That would give them all equal amounts."

"Yeah, I guess. Why?"

"Just thinking. If three boys are picking up bottles along the road or in the park or wherever, it's strange they would always get the same amount each. Three boys would probably make it a contest to see who could get the most. Wouldn't you think so?"

There was a silence in the near-empty restaurant. And when Mabel didn't answer, Vic turned to look at her and prompt her.

"Well, wouldn't you?"

"I see what you mean, Mr. Princeton. You think there's something fishy going on."

"Tell Tootie, when he comes in to clean tonight, to count all the empties out back and put a note on my desk. And then keep a count of how many you take back to the alley each evening."

"Count every bottle? You want us to count every empty bottle every time?"

"It won't be that many, and it won't be that long. Just do it for the next day or so, and then I don't think we'll have to do it anymore."

"All right. Tootie won't like having something extra to do, but I'll tell him. He'll grumble and gripe about it."

"That's okay," Vic said as he went back to his table and picked up his coffee cup. "He'll get over it."

At Tootie's first count that Friday night, there were sixty-seven empty Coca-Cola bottles in the alley by the kitchen door of Mulligans. By 3:00 p.m. Saturday, there were seventy-four. Most of Mulligans' soft drink sales were fountain drinks, which were served in paper cups for lunch and glasses for dinner. Vic Princeton was just hanging up the phone after

putting in a food order to the regional wholesaler for a Monday morning
delivery when the front door opened and three boys stepped in with paper
sacks in their hands. He knew two of them but recognized all three as the
bottle boys from the day before. He turned to a young waitress who was
wiping down a table and said, "Nancy, go out back real quick and count
the empties. Hurry up, and I'll explain later."

"We have some more bottles," the tallest boy said to Mabel, who was
standing at the register, having just rung up a couple who was leaving.

"Already? You were just here yesterday. How many do you have now?"

Before they could answer, Vic came out of the back and intercepted
the transaction.

"Good afternoon, gentlemen. What could I help you with?"

"We, uh, were just, uh, talking to Miss Talley about some bottles,"
Cal answered quickly.

"Bottles? You've got bottles in those bags?"

"Yes sir."

"Where'd you get them?"

"Out along the road and over at the ballpark under the bleachers,"
Cal lied.

"It's terrible the way people throw things out along the road, isn't it?
You find a lot of broken ones, I'll bet."

"Yes sir. Sometimes."

"Cal, do you always do all the talking for these guys?"

"No sir. Not always. They can talk, too, sometimes."

"That's good. I know one of your friends here. You're the Stone boy,
aren't you? H. V.'s boy?"

"Yes sir."

"But you, son, I don't know. What's your name?"

"*Buddy.*"

"*I see. Well, fellows, I'm going to make you a little bet. I'm going to bet you that I can guess how many bottles you each have in your bag. And if I get it right, I don't owe you a thing. But if I get it wrong, I'll pay you double. How about that?*"

The three boys looked at one another, confused about how to react to such a deal. Oddly, it was Buddy who spoke first.

"*Why?*"

"*Why? Because I'm a gambler. I gamble on the golf course. I gamble in the stock market. I gamble all the time. So I'm gambling that I can guess how many bottles you have. Deal?*"

"*Okay. It's a deal,*" *Cal said with a grin all over his face.*

"*I thought you'd be the first to take me up on it, Cal. You're an enterprising young lad. How about you other fellows?*"

"*That goes for all of us,*" *Cal said with confidence.*

Nancy came in from the kitchen and whispered quietly to Vic, "Fifty-nine."

Vic looked down at the boys and said, "Buddy, you have five. Mr. Stone, you have five. And Little Cal, you also have five. Put them right up here on this table and count them out."

The boys were stunned and silent, and none of them made a move to empty their bags. For a moment, Vic thought they might break and run, but in time it was, of course, Cal who spoke up.

"*How did you know that? How did you know how many we each had?*"

Vic took the bags from each boy, one at a time, and sat them on the table. He motioned for them to come over and sit down, and by the time they reached their chairs, all three faces were drained of any color the autumn wind and sun might have given them that day. "You three little bilkers have been stealing my bottles from the alley and coming in here and selling them back to me. No telling how much money you owe me."

"How do you know that we've been …?" Cal started to ask.

"No. No. Don't make it worse by denying it. You did it. You got caught. You take the consequences. That's the way a man does it. Now the only thing we have to work out is what we're going to do about it."

The boys were silent and scared. This tall giant of a man was standing staring down at them and somehow he knew exactly what they had been doing. All three felt an urge to cry but didn't want the other two to see him do it.

"I see three possible solutions to the matter. I can call the police, and heaven knows what they might do. Come lock you up, I suppose. Or I can call your parents. And I think I know what they will do. Even though I don't know yours, Buddy, I think I can guess they will handle it pretty much the way H. V. and Ernest will. Or … or I could … no, you wouldn't want to do that."

"Do what?" It was Cal again, but the other two faces asked the same question.

"Or I could let you work it off. Instead of going to the picture show on Saturdays or whatever it is you do that day, you could come in here and work for me."

"Doing what?"

"Doing whatever I say. You might wash dishes or mop the floor. You might wait on tables or take the trash out. Just whatever needs to be done from about ten until three o'clock for the next three Saturdays."

"Three Saturdays? Why three Saturdays?" Cal asked for the group.

"*Because there're three of you. I think that would be as good a number as any. Or I could count up how many bottles you've stolen over the past few weeks and use that number.*"

"*No, that's all right. Three Saturdays will be okay with us,*" Cal quickly added.

And so they came. And for the next three Saturdays, they were at the mercy of Vic Princeton, Mt. Jefferson's reigning celebrity—or slave master, depending on your personal perspective.

CHAPTER TWENTY-THREE

Buddy and Cal stood just outside the curtained cubicle until Darcy peeped out and invited them inside. Harlan was awake and seemingly aware of his surroundings and condition.

"He's doing fine. The nurse said you could talk to him for just a few minutes, and then they're going to take him up to his room. He'll be on the third floor."

"Thanks. Why don't you go out and sit with Amanda for a few minutes while we say a word to him?" Buddy suggested.

"I can't stay back here while you two talk to him? What are you going to ask him? You know now, Buddy, he's in no shape to be answering a lot of questions."

"I understand that. But I have just a couple of things, and then we'll be right out."

"I'm not sure I like this much. I thought you were coming back here to check on him as a friend. Not interrogate him as a police officer. He's just not up to it."

"Darcy, don't get upset," Cal consoled. "There're just some things

Buddy needs to say to him and he needs to say to Buddy. Why don't you and I go out and sit down for just a couple of minutes while they talk."

"No," Buddy said sharply. "I want you to stay, Cal. We won't be but a few minutes, Darcy."

Buddy just stared her down and waited for her to leave without any further explaining or coaxing. Cal was seeing him become who he was on the job for the first time in all the years he'd known him. There was a different and keener air about him—something much more official—and Cal never took his eyes off of him as Darcy pushed through the curtains and disappeared.

"You okay, pal?" Buddy asked, looking down at Harlan.

"Yeah, I'm going to be all right. What was wrong with her staying?" Harlan asked.

"I just wanted you to tell me what happened, and I wanted you to be totally free to say whatever you needed to say."

Buddy's actions would have seemed harsh to an outsider, but they were of the warmest possible nature. He felt there might be a chance this intruder had something to do with a side of Harlan's life that Darcy might not be privy to. He didn't know of anything for sure, but he knew it wasn't outside the realm of possibility, and Buddy was just giving him the freedom of honesty among old friends.

"I got nothing to hide from her. It is what it is. Some clown busted in my house and shot me. And I really do mean a clown."

"From the front."

"I see. Just like on television." Harlan looked to his left where Cal was standing. "Are you going to take notes like Frank Smith to his Joe Friday?"

"No." Cal smiled. "But I am going to hang around to make sure he doesn't beat you up too badly."

"I'm not going to beat anybody up," Buddy said with a slight smile. "I just want to know what happened over there this morning."

"Darcy said she already told you. We heard a noise. We went downstairs...."

"What kind of noise?"

"You know, like somebody kicking in the back door."

"Okay. Go ahead."

"We went downstairs and there he was in the kitchen."

"Who was?"

"The guy. The guy that broke in the door."

"Describe him."

"Oh, I don't know. He had a mask. Like a circus clown. And that's about all I can tell you about him."

"What was he doing?"

"Doing? He wasn't doing anything. He was just there in the kitchen."

"Hunched over?"

"What?"

"Was he hunched over?"

Harlan frowned and then grimaced. "Yeah, I reckon."

"Did he say anything?"

"Yeah, I think so, but I don't know what. Didn't she tell you all this?"

The nurse from earlier, Kathy Foster, stepped inside the curtain.

"Sorry to break up this party, gentlemen, but we have Mr. Stone's room ready. If you'll give us about twenty minutes, we'll have him upstairs in room 324, and you can both come up as soon as the doctor says it's okay."

Cal took Harlan's hand. "I'll wait and talk to you up there. It won't be long."

Harlan managed a smile and said, "Thanks, guys, for being here. I really need you both. And you don't have any idea how much."

Cal and Buddy walked back down the hallway toward the waiting area but stopped short of going through the double doors to where Darcy and Amanda were sitting.

"I thought you didn't want me to be in there when you questioned him."

"I changed my mind."

"Why?"

"Because I realized I might need you."

"You're not making any sense, Buddy."

"I'm not sure I can trust everything I might hear. And I need you there to validate it."

Cal looked at his friend for a long moment with Buddy unblinkingly returning the stare. And just before pushing through the big double doors, Cal said, "If I understood what you were trying to say, I might argue with you. But until I do, I'll keep my mouth shut."

CHAPTER TWENTY-FOUR

The next three Saturdays were hard work for the little bottle boys. The only work any of them had ever done was a few chores around the house. But at eleven years old, none had ever experienced anything like working on a schedule. And on their day off from school. They had fretted all week over losing the freedom of their Saturdays—of not being able to go to the movies, and then not having the freedom to decide if they would roam the streets all Saturday afternoon or ride their bikes around the neighborhood. The humiliation reached its peak that first Saturday at 10:00 a.m. when they walked in and Vic tossed each of them an apron.

"What's this for?" Cal asked.

"For you to wear. What do you think it's for?" Vic asked with no sign of a smile.

He was playing this out for all it was worth. He could see the boys sweating and knew that each new wrinkle he made them accept in their agreement was just driving the lesson home. He wanted to laugh as he watched them put the apron straps around their necks and then attempted to tie the sashes behind their backs. But he kept a rigid face with the boys and only showed his smile to Mabel Talley when they weren't looking.

Everything went without a hitch until about twelve thirty that first day. Little Cal was washing dishes, Buddy was emptying garbage and stacking bottles out back—of all things—and Harlan was trying to look busy doing nothing when four orders came ready at the same time in the kitchen. Vic picked up a plate with a bowl of chicken noodle soup from the metal steam table by the cook's station and said, "Harlan. Here. Take this soup out to the man in that first booth on the left. And don't spill it."

Harlan wanted to balk at first. None of the three had told anyone about what they were doing and the punishment they were receiving—especially their parents. They had figured if they could stay in the kitchen, no one would ever know they were working there. The only way it could get out would be if Vic told his sister Betty Bell. Cal was willing to take this chance, so they had agreed to try to keep it all a secret from their families. But now here he stood with a bowl of soup in his hands. What if his father was out there? Or Cal's father or mother? Or Buddy's parents? Or anyone else who might know them? He closed his eyes, took a deep breath, pushed through the swinging door, and walked, without looking left or right, straight to the first booth on the left. But as he set the bowl of steaming soup on the table in front of the lone customer, he looked up into the face of someone he had never expected to see. He froze, and without saying a word, turned quickly on his heel and nearly ran back into the kitchen.

"We're in trouble," Harlan whispered to Buddy.

"What do you mean?"

"Out there in the booth. Look out there."

Cal saw them with their heads together and then standing on the tip of their toes, peeping through the kitchen door leading into the dining room.

"What's wrong?" he asked. "Who's out there?"

And then all three were standing in a cluster, scanning the eating area via the door window.

"Out of my way, boys. Food coming through," Mabel said as she pushed between them with one hand, a large tray of plates balanced on the palm of the other. "Don't stand in the doorway, or you'll get run over. And don't forget. Any plates and glasses you break, you pay for."

Saturday night at ten minutes after nine, as Vic Princeton locked the back door of Mulligans, pulled his suit collar up around his neck, and walked through the alley toward his 1927 Whippet, a figure stepped out of the shadows from behind the garbage cans. Startled, Vic stopped short, as he couldn't make out any facial features. That it was a man was all he could assume. That, and the fact that he was nearly a full foot shorter, was as much as he could be sure of until the man spoke.

"Princeton."

"Yes?"

"The Stone boy."

"Harlan. What about him?"

"Why he be working for you?"

"Fritz? Is that you?"

"That be me. Why about the boy?"

"It's a long story, Fritz. Just a little lesson I'm teaching those boys." Vic chuckled.

"Not funny. H. V. Stone's boy should not be in your kitchen. Not right and proper for that boy."

"Did you tell his dad about it? I had thought about telling him, but I didn't want to get the boys in any more trouble. Did you say anything to him?"

"Not your business what I do. But it be my business what you do. Fire him."

"I can't do that, Fritz. I'm trying to teach these boys a lesson."

"Don't make me teach you a lesson. Fire him. Kitchen is no place for H. V.'s boy."

"Fritz, I don't think you understand. I just want ..."

"Do it."

Fritz's shadow stretched from its five feet six inches to twelve feet as he disappeared under the street lamp and out of sight. Vic stood and watched him go. He pulled a cigarette from his shirt pocket, lit it, and blew out a stream of smoke. He yelled into the silence as the alley echoed, "Good night, Fritz. Good talking to you."

CHAPTER TWENTY-FIVE

Buddy sent Amanda home and Darcy upstairs to room 324 to wait for Harlan's arrival. This left only Cal and him in the waiting room.

"What are you going to do?" Buddy asked, stretching his back.

"I think I'll go home, shower, and put on some decent clothes. You?"

"I'll stop at the phone down here and call the station. See what's new." Looking at his watch, Buddy asked, "What time are you coming back?"

"It's nearly eight thirty now, so I should be back by ten."

"Then so will I. We'll go up together and talk to him."

"Buddy, what are you expecting to hear?"

"I'm not sure. And I'm not lying to you. It's just an instinct I have about these things. I don't know how to explain it or what to compare it to in your line of work."

"I think I do. Sometimes I walk into a home for one reason or another, and I can sense the mood that's in there. If the man and wife are happy or if their teenager is giving them a fit. It's a reading and a gut feeling you can't define."

"Exactly. You should have been a cop. And maybe that's why I want you there. I want to be real sure on this one. I'll need your instincts."

"I'll see you right back here at ten."

Buddy went to the same phone booth Cal had sat in just an hour before and dialed the police station.

"Mt. Jefferson Police. Sergeant Kesterton."

"Carl, this is Briggs. Put me through to Sikes."

"Sure thing, Lieutenant."

There was a short wait and some clicking on the line, then a pickup.

"Buddy. How's your pal?"

"Doing good. Out of surgery. Looks like nothing too serious."

"A gunshot wound is always serious. I've been there, friend, and it hurts."

To someone listening who didn't know, this might sound like the heartfelt confession of a hero. But what Miland Sikes was actually referring to was the time his stewed-to-the-gills uncle shot him in the leg with buckshot in a duck blind at North Mountain Lake. Sometimes just hearing the truth isn't enough—you have to know the truth too.

"You got anything back from the scene yet?" Buddy asked.

"Sure do. We got prints. Good ones. I need to print Harlan and his wife and even his kids if they don't mind. That way we can eliminate."

"His kids aren't here. Skip them. Go over to the hospital and get his and hers. Room 324. Tell them I said it's okay. Then get something we can run through the system just as fast as possible."

"Will do."

"And, hey, Sikes—what about the door? I was over there earlier, and everything was swept clean."

"That was us. He busted in the lock. Looks like he used his foot. He wasn't trying to come in quiet. He was there, and he didn't care who knew it."

"Any kind of sole or heel markings?"

"Nah. Just a big ole black smudge where he hit it like he was trying to come through it."

"Okay. Thanks, Miland. I'll be in by noon. Good work."

CHAPTER TWENTY-SIX

Nine-thirty Monday morning saw Vic Princeton in his ivy driving cap and lightweight tan overcoat, coming out of Vaxter Brothers Hardware Store. He was smiling and speaking to everyone he met and was even stopping and talking to those who bade him more than just a "good morning." His destination was three doors down, but he was in no particular hurry to get there. He had often philosophized that every hand he shook was a potential customer. And his theory had proven favorable for many years. He never turned away a fan or cut short a compliment. He loved the adoration as much as the compensation. He was still waving and flashing a winning smile to all on Main Street as he pushed on the glass door to Stones by Stone Jewelers.

"H. V. Stone. The man who greases the wheel of fortune for all of Mt. Jefferson."

"Vic. How's the boy. How's the boy."

They shook hands vigorously, as if an important negotiation was about to take place. And maybe it was.

"Now don't tell me, Vic, that you've come in for that diamond engagement ring. Has some bright and beautiful damsel got her hooks into you, finally?"

"Not a chance, H. V. Not a chance. I'm certified and confirmed. A bachelor to my dying day."

"Aw, come on, Vic. Never say never. You don't know what cute little filly may be around the corner who just might catch your fancy. And your pocketbook."

This brought guffaws from them both and ended the small talk. By this time, H. V. was wondering why he really was in the store, and Vic was ready to set into motion the reason for his visit.

"What brings you in this morning, my boy?"

"Your son."

"Harlan? What's he done? Something I'm going to be ashamed of or proud of?"

"Well, it's not like that at all. I see him and those two little friends of his running up and down the street all the time, and I was just wondering if you thought they might like to have a job."

"A job? The boy is eleven years old."

"You and I can remember how good it felt when we were kids to have a little pocket money of our own. Buy some candy and some pop. I got odd jobs around the restaurant that need to be done all the time, and I could use those boys for a few hours on Saturdays to clean up a little and take out the trash—maybe even wash a few dishes to give my man a little time off. I just thought I'd check with you to make sure it would be all right for me to talk to Harlan."

"Well, I don't see why not. It would do the boy good to have a little responsibility. You know, he's a good boy. He'll do you a good job."

"I'm sure he will. I talked to Ernest just now about Little Cal, and they gave me the name of the Briggs boy's parents. I'll find them. But I wanted to clear it with you. And to tell you the truth," Vic said as he dropped his voice and leaned in a little closer, "it will save me a dime or two not having to hire an adult and will help the boys in their self-esteem at the same time."

"Vic, you're a good man. That's good thinking, and I think those boys will jump at the chance."

"Then it's a deal. I'll talk to them this week. And how is everything with you here at the store?"

"Peaches and cream."

"That's great. Give your wife my best. And also Fritz. How is old Fritz? Is he here?"

"Yeah, he's there in the back. He won't ever come out front."

Vic raised his voice, "Fritz, if you can hear me. Good morning, and have a great day!"

H. V. and Vic laughed again when there was no response from the back and then walked down the aisle to the door, arm in arm. Neither of them saw Fritz come to the curtain that led to the back room and look out as H. V. stood at the door, waving at Vic, who was walking down the street again with his coat blowing in the wind.

CHAPTER TWENTY-SEVEN

"Hello." She sounded sleepy.

"Shirley Ann? Did I wake you?" Buddy asked, knowing he had.

"No."

"Are you sure?"

"Well, yeah, you did, but that's all right."

"I'm sorry. I just wanted to check on you. Mamma told me you were feeling a little blue this morning. But no pains, huh?"

"No. I sort of wish there were. I think I'm ready to have this over with."

"Oh, believe me, it won't be over with. It's just getting started."

"You know what I mean, Daddy." She laughed. "How about you? How's Uncle Harlan?"

"He's going to be all right."

"Can you tell me what happened, or is that police secrets?"

"You can't have secrets till you know something. And we really don't know anything yet. But what about you? Can I do anything for you?"

"Yeah, you can. Quit worrying. Louis Wayne can be here in ten minutes if anything happens. I'll be just fine."

"I can be there in ten minutes too."

The silence on the other end told Buddy he should have kept that last thought a rumbling in his head instead of letting it escape from his mouth. It seemed that more and more of their conversations had these awkward moments of late. Amanda was right. Shirley Ann was no longer his, and he was no longer the first person on her mind when she had a need. She had a husband who stood between them now, and every passing day was a rude reminder. Buddy would have to deal with it. There was no alternative anyway. The decision had been made for him.

"Mamma has gone home, so if you need her she'll be there all day. I've got to go now. Take care."

"Okay, Daddy. Bye."

Buddy pushed the folding door open but sat in the phone booth for a few more moments. He would have to leave this problem in the hands of his daughter and his wife and concentrate on the job at hand. The problem with the job at hand was how to separate the personal from the business. In the meantime, he would go to the cafeteria and eat breakfast. By that time, Cal would be back. He apparently sat there staring straight ahead and thinking longer than he was aware because the next thing he realized was that an orderly was standing in front of him.

"Are you finished? I need to make a call."

"Sure. It's all yours."

When the automatic door opened and Cal walked in, Buddy moved to the elevator and pushed the number three button. They said nothing on the way up, as the car was full of people, all politely quiet. Buddy was always annoyed by people who liked to carry on a conversation in an elevator while other people stood by, looking at the ceiling and listening to every word. Neither man spoke until they had turned the corner in the hallway that led to Harlan's room.

"You want to go first?" Buddy asked before entering the room.

"No. It's your show. I'll be there for you. And you can stay when I take over. You probably haven't had a prayer yet this morning anyway."

"Don't count on it, preacher man. In my job every minute is a prayer."

"You know what? I believe that."

Cal patted him on the back as they entered the room.

Darcy stood up from the chair beside the bed when she saw them coming. "I suppose you want me to leave again."

"Darcy. Don't start," Harlan said from his prone position, wide awake.

"Okay. I'll go get some coffee. Do either of you want any?" she asked.

"No, thanks," Cal said. Buddy just shook his head no.

When she had cleared the room, Buddy closed the door behind her.

"How you feel, pal?" Cal asked.

"Sore, whipped, and mad." Harlan said through clenched teeth.

"That's normal, I'm sure."

"I mean, all I can think about is that some guy broke into my house in the middle of the night and here I am in the shape I'm in and I didn't do anything to deserve it."

"We don't always get what we deserve in life. Get over that idea."

"Yeah, that's easy for you to say." Harlan seemed to regret he had said this the second his words hit the air. "I'm sorry, Cal. I didn't mean that. Lord knows, life's no bowl of cherries for you."

"Forget it."

"Who was the guy?" Buddy spoke for the first time, but his tone communicated that he was now in charge.

"I don't know who he was," Harlan assured him.

"Then you know why he was there."

"No, I don't."

"Who've you made mad lately? Who's got it in for you?"

"Nobody."

"Don't lie to me, Harlan. I'm not stupid. I do live in this town, you know. Not everybody here loves you. Who's after you?"

"What's up with you? A burglar broke into my house and shot me, and you're trying to make me responsible?"

"I'm trying to find out the truth."

"You think I'm lying to you?"

"Don't make me answer that. You're one of the best friends I have in the world. The other one is standing beside me. I don't have many secrets from either one of you. You know that. So I'm asking you as a friend. Who do you owe? Who's out to get you?"

Harlan closed his eyes for a long time. Nothing and nobody in the room moved. When he finally opened them, he looked Buddy solidly in both his eyes and said, "Why don't you think it was simply a burglar?"

"Why don't you give credit to every bumpkin that comes in off the street and wants to buy a silver bracelet?"

"What?"

"Instincts. You know who to trust. And I think you trusted the wrong person."

Harlan turned his face away from Buddy, shutting him out completely, and said, "Cal, I think you came in here to have a prayer. If you did, get on with it so I can get some sleep. I've just been shot and had major surgery, for God's sake."

Chapter Twenty-Eight

With the full permission of their parents, the boys worked off their debt over the next two Saturdays. At the end of the last Saturday afternoon on the job, Vic called them back to his little office just off the dining room. They squeezed in, closed the door, and stood around his desk, not knowing what to expect.

"You are three of the most trying little devils I have ever seen in my life. You sneak around and steal from me. But you know what? You got caught, and you stood up and took it like a general. And what really bowled me over was you did good work. All of you. Not a slacker among you. So here's what I'm going to do. Your parents are going to wonder where the money is you've been earning ..."

"Mine's already asked," Cal interrupted. "I told them you hadn't paid us yet."

"What are you going to tell them the next time they ask?"

They looked at one another with blank expressions.

"I don't know. Tell them we spent it, I reckon," Cal answered.

"You won't have to lie to your mammas and daddies. Here's three dollars for each of you," Vic said, handing them their money.

"*Three dollars! You kidding? We can keep this?*" *Cal asked.*

"*All yours.*"

"*I don't think it's right, Mr. Princeton.*" *It was Buddy speaking this time.*

Cal and Harlan turned and looked at their friend so quickly they nearly bumped each other over.

"*Shut up,*" *Cal demanded.*

"*No. Let him talk,*" *Vic said, leaning back in his chair.*

"*I don't know. It's just that we did something wrong, and this was our punishment—and you even fixed it so our parents wouldn't find out. And now you're giving us money. It don't feel right.*"

"*You want to give it back to me?*"

"*I don't want to,*" *Buddy admitted. "But I know I should. So, yeah, I guess I will.*" *He laid his three dollars on the edge of Vic's desk.*

Harlan reluctantly followed suit. Cal was the last to react. But just before he made the gesture, placing his on the growing stack of money, he boldly said, "Uncle Vic, how about we give you two back and keep one. That seems fair, don't it?"

Vic Princeton threw his head back, and the booming laugh that came through the closed door made all the patrons turn their heads to see what the amusement was all about.

"*You are downright good boys. Some of you better than others, but all in all, good boys. How would you like to come in here and work every Saturday for a couple of hours?*"

"*For money?*" *Harlan asked.*

"*Sure, for money. Just like a real job.*"

There were smiles and head shakes all around the room. The boys were laughing now just as loudly as their boss. The meeting was over, and all had conquered. And a relationship to last a lifetime had commenced.

"Here, boys. Take your money back. You earned it in more ways than one. And I'll say it again. You are three of the most charming little mulligans I could ever hope to meet. If anybody ever deserved another chance, you three are it. Now get out of here, and go spend that money."

They did. And every Saturday until they were well into their teens, they came to work and tied on their aprons and proudly took their places as employees of Mulligans, one of the finer restaurants in all of Mt. Jefferson. Even after they outgrew the jobs, they often visited Mulligans to eat in the last booth in the back on the right. When they started dating they brought their girlfriends there—sometimes for dinner and sometimes just for a soda after the movies, depending on how often they could scrape together the money. They came in all combinations—together, in pairs, or alone; after school in the evenings and after church on Sunday just to hang out. But whenever they came, there was one constant: the love and respect they showed for the man who had taken the time to give them the time of day. His lesson and his friendship were cherished by all three of them, and their secret was kept forever. Anybody stealing bottles from Uncle Vic now had the Mulligans to answer to.

BUDDY BRIGGS

CHAPTER TWENTY-NINE

Very few people ever knew his real name. The kids he went to school with, the girls he dated, the guys in the army, the people he worked with—they all just knew him as Buddy, and he was the type of man one just never thought of pushing for a real name. He not only wore his nickname well, but he became his nickname. It was given to him by his mother, who felt a certain amount of guilt for putting his full moniker on her helpless little baby. To name him after his grandfathers seemed like such a wonderful idea until the actual time came to fill out the birth certificate. Then it was too late to come up with something more suitable, so she and her husband just closed their eyes and held their breath and uttered the official order that christened their one and only son Wendall Forester Briggs. At no point in his life could he ever remember anyone actually calling him either of his legal names. Even when his mother was angry at him, she never resorted to "Wendall Forester Briggs! Get in this house this minute!" as so many mothers do. His real names were used so seldom that the few times he had to write them—on insurance papers and income tax forms—he always found the capital W *and* F *awkward to form. He was Buddy to one and all at all times.*

Eileen and Chub Briggs were the solid middle-class people the country was built on and thrived on. Chub was a fireman and also ran an Esso station that sat kitty-corner across the street from the firehouse. Some of Buddy's earliest memories were of spending the day at the service station with his dad, helping wash the windshields and sitting on the drink box, eating peanuts and candy bars.

Countering all the good memories of the New Street Esso were the times the fire bell would ring in the firehouse tower and make his ears hurt. But he would always love standing on the curb and watching his dad run across the street—and then, after what seemed like mere seconds of anxious waiting, watching the fire truck pull out into the waiting traffic with all the noise and clang it could muster. Buddy would pace the time away in the driveway while ole Major, the black mechanic, watched out the bay doors every few minutes to make sure he was okay. Sometimes after hours of waiting, Buddy would finally see the grille of the old fire engine chugging around the corner, and his dad, covered in soot and sweat, would wave to him from the back of the truck. Then something happened the summer he turned six that twisted this into a bad memory. Arlie Paine, a good friend of Chub's, had gone out on the call with the other firefighters but didn't come back with them. Buddy remembered sitting at the top of the stairs in his pajamas and listening to his dad tell his mother about how the flames had shot up through the ceiling of a house when they weren't expecting it. The flames had caught Arlie Paine by surprise, and he never made it out. Chub's voice was as close to crying as Buddy had ever heard. Buddy could only picture what he expected were tears running down his dad's face.

From that day on, the sudden ringing of the fire alarm didn't bring the excitement it used to for Buddy. Instead, it brought fear. More than once he could remember watching his dad hang on to the back of the fire truck as it made its way out of the big doors until it disappeared down the street. But instead of biding his time on the curb while ole Major watched out for him, Buddy would hide in the storeroom among the cases of oil and try to block the fears from his little mind.

"You in here, Buddy?" Major called.

"Yes sir."

"Where are you?"

"Back here in the corner."

Major stepped over a few boxes and then sat down on one of them and pulled a greasy rag from his hip pocket. He took off his Esso cap and wiped the dampness from the inside band.

"Your daddy's going to be all right. No need for you to fret like this. He been going out on these fire runs for years, long 'fore you were born, and he ain't never been hurt yet."

"What about Mr. Paine?"

"Mr. Paine had some bad luck, boy. And bad luck ain't something we can fend ourself against. Your daddy can take care of hisself."

"Not if a fire shoots up when he ain't expecting it. He could burn up just like Mr. Paine."

"Son, I have fellow feeling for Arlie Paine and all his family. But even they wouldn't want you to lay around and pine the way you doing. Now come on out here, and let's watch for that old red truck. It'll be coming around that corner 'fore you know it."

"Major?"

"What's that, boy?"

"Is that what hell's like? Fire and all?"

"Hell ain't always fire, son. Hell is different things to different folks. And you know what? Hell is sometimes just sitting around worrying about things you got no dominion over. Now get out here and get you a soda pop and a Baby Ruth. I got work to do."

Chub Briggs always came back, and Buddy was always waiting for him. And ole Major was forever peeping out one of those bays, making sure all the world was right for both of them.

CHAPTER THIRTY

"Go ahead and say it."

"Say what? What do you want me to say?" Cal asked.

"Just what you're thinking. That I was too hard on him."

"You've got your job to do. I'm not going to tell you how to do it."

"Yeah, but you don't like the way I'm handling it, do you?"

"Buddy, are you looking for someone to fight with? Do you want me to take issue with the way you're handling things so you'll have somebody to strike out at? Is that what this is all about?"

Buddy took a long, deep breath and let it out with an audible sigh before he spoke again. "Maybe so. And maybe you should have been a head doctor instead of a spirit doctor. I was too hard on him, wasn't I?"

"He can take it. But I would like to know what you have in mind. What you're basing all these assumptions on."

"You've been away for a while and haven't kept your ear to the track the way I have. It's a small town, and you hear things. It's my business to know what's going on here. And just between you and me—it's nothing I can even come close to proving—but I think Harlan has been having some trouble with the Drakos family."

"Nick? The old man?"

"Maybe. Maybe Nicoli. Maybe Christopher. I don't know. But I'm pretty sure there is some bad blood there."

"I haven't seen Nicoli since I've been back. I saw Christopher just last week."

"And?"

"And he was Christopher. What can I say? Just as arrogant as he was when he was sixteen years old. Hasn't grown up or changed much at all. What about Nicoli?"

"We've got a sheet on him as long as the Shenandoah River. And just about as crooked. I worry that Harlan is tied up with them in some way."

"Gambling?"

Just as Cal asked this question and before Buddy could answer, two women walked past them, chatting as they went in the front doors of Lenity General.

"I guess standing in front of the hospital is no place to be having this conversation. You want to go someplace we can talk?" Cal asked.

"Sure. Let's meet for lunch at ... what do you say, one o'clock? I've got to go back by the station."

"I'll see you at one."

That neither Cal nor Buddy specified where they would meet for lunch was an observation almost anyone overhearing their parting remarks would have made. But it was unnecessary for them to confirm that after all these years. At one o'clock, less than a minute before Buddy arrived, Cal was sitting in the last booth in the back on the right at Mulligans, sipping sweet iced tea and talking with Vic Princeton. Vic stood up when Buddy arrived and hugged him as he always did.

"Uncle Vic. Keep your seat."

"Nah. I was just sitting here chewing the fat with the reverend till you got here. I'll leave you two boys to yourselves."

"No, I'm serious. I'd like for you to stay."

"Really? A stooped-over, old white-headed codger like me?"

"Certainly, Uncle Vic," Cal said. "We figure if you stay, you'll buy. And we'll put up with anything for a free lunch."

"Now you're sounding like the old Cal." And Vic slapped Buddy on the back as he scooted back into the booth, all three of them laughing. "I was just asking Cal here how your other partner is. What a shock when I heard that this morning."

"He's going to be all right," Buddy assured him. "That's what this lunch is about. That's why I wanted you to stay."

"Sounds serious, boys," Vic said as he pulled a Pall Mall pack from his shirt pocket. "Tell Uncle Vic all about it."

CHAPTER THIRTY-ONE

Eileen Briggs taught the sixth grade at Hanna Cole Elementary from the time she was fresh out of teacher's college. The only leave of absence she ever took was when Buddy was born and then again when his little sister, Charlotte, came into the world. She instilled a work ethic in each of her children that would not only get them through their schooling with honorable grades but also take them through life with a responsible attitude. Apart from her teaching career and her job as homemaker and mother, Eileen made all of her own clothes and most of Charlotte's. She taught a Sunday school class and still found time to read all the new novels that appealed to her. Buddy often said of her in later years that she was the only person he had ever known who had actually read all the classics so many claim to have read. She had covered all those titles while still in high school and college and after that mostly read for pleasure. Chub didn't share any of those interests with her, and many who knew them wondered just what their attraction to each other really was. They were opposites on so many fronts and yet appeared to be extremely happy to all who were close to them.

Eileen was in the teachers' lounge finishing a chapter in Edna Ferber's So Big while her friend Fran Peers, a fifth grade teacher, sat grading papers. The door opened, and they both recognized the woman who entered with a flourish and sat down next to them. Her name was Barbara Bowls. She was known to all the students as Miz Bowls and was the floating music teacher for all the county grade schools. Every month she would go from school to school and room to room and hold a thirty-minute session in each. She carried a pitch pipe and taught silly little songs to all those willing to learn. Mostly she got stares from the little boys and giggles from the little girls, but she was young and pretty, in a shallow sort of way, and was able to get by with the things she had to do.

"Good morning, ladies. I hope you don't mind if I join you," Barbara Bowls said dropping into a chair.

"Not at all. Make yourself at home," Eileen said, looking up from her book.

"Do either of you mind if I smoke?"

"Smoke?" Eileen repeated as Fran looked up from her papers.

"I know. I know. Everybody frowns on women who like to take a little puff now and then. I picked up the habit in college. Now don't tell me neither one of you never tried it once or twice?"

"I'm afraid I'd have to tell you just that," Eileen said with no malice or judgment in her voice.

"What about you, sister? You going to look down your nose too?"

Before Fran Peers could defend herself, Eileen spoke up again with the book still open in her lap.

"No one is looking down their nose at you, deary. I simply answered your question. Why don't you just light up and relax and try not to be so defensive about what you're doing."

"I'm not ... well, yes ... I guess I am defensive, aren't I? I have to sneak around, or everybody just thinks I'm the bride of the devil if I light up in public. I guess I just thought you two would think the same. I'm so sorry."

"It's okay," Eileen assured her.

"Have we met?" Barbara asked as she exhaled a stream of blue smoke.

"We have. I'm Mrs. Briggs from the sixth grade, and this is Mrs. Peers from the fifth."

"How do you do, ladies? I do hope I haven't made you mad. I am just so ... well ... I don't know what. This schedule they have me on is driving me daffy. I wish I could stay in one place the way you do. I can't do this the rest of my life."

"How long have you been teaching?" Fran asked, speaking for the first time.

"This is my first year. But I'm quitting as soon as I can. I can't stand it much longer."

"What do you plan to do?"

"Oh, I'll still teach. But just not at school. What I want to do is teach piano. Have a little studio somewhere in town and have the students come to me instead of me running all over the county to them. And no voice teaching. I hate that. Just piano. That's my dream."

"I think that's such a sweet talent," Fran said. "I always wished I had learned to play."

"It's not too late, you know. I could teach you and have you playing songs in two months."

"Oh, no. I could never do that."

"You should try, Fran," Eileen said. "You'd learn fast and be good at it, I'm sure."

"Oh, heavens, no. I could never do that now. I don't know where I'd ever find the time. But you know what I'd really like? I'd really like for my little girl to learn to play. What is a good age for them to start?" Fran asked Miz Bowls.

"Can she read?" Barbara asked, waving a cloud of smoke away from her face.

"Oh, certainly she can. She's in the third grade."

"Then she's ready and ripe. I could start her tomorrow."

"Really? Where would you teach her?"

"In my apartment on the top of New Street hill. Anytime after school from about three to six. Whatever would suit you. A lesson is thirty minutes long."

"How much does it cost?"

"One lesson a week. A dollar a lesson. And she'll be playing 'Sweet Betsy From Pike' with both hands by Thanksgiving."

Fran looked at Eileen and said, "Oh, I'm so tempted to say yes. Do you think I should?"

"Do it," Eileen encouraged her.

"Only one problem. We don't have a piano."

"Well, she'll need a piano to practice on. The lessons would be useless if she couldn't practice," Miz Bowls said, flicking her ashes.

"I don't know, then. I guess it just wouldn't work."

"Fran, you know what?" Eileen asked excitedly. "We have a piano in the parlor. Your daughter could come over and practice at our house anytime she wanted. Matter of fact, I'd love for someone to be using it. It's just sitting there wasting away."

Fran turned back to Miz Bowls. "How often would she have to practice?"

"I tell my students they need to practice every day. But nobody does. If she gets in twenty minutes a week, believe me, that's more than most of the little scamps who have one perched in their living room." Miz Bowls was grounding out her cigarette in a glass ashtray the whole time she was saying this.

"Eileen, are you sure? Are you sure your husband wouldn't mind?"

"Heavens, no. He's never home till eight o'clock anyway. She wouldn't be bothering a soul."

And that's how it happened.

The first time he saw her was through the screen door as she was walking up their front walk with her practice book under her arm. Eight-year-old Buddy Briggs stood in the hall and watched eight-year-old Amanda Peers ring the doorbell. He was too shy to answer it, so he hid behind a bureau while his mother came to the door and ushered the little girl to the parlor and showed her the piano. Two days a week after school for the next two and a half years, Amanda came and practiced her scales and then her songs. Soon Buddy was answering the door and then lounging on the footstool while she played, and by the time the Peers bought their own piano, he was sorry to see her go. But she wasn't gone from his life for long. They talked on the telephone, found each other at school, and were holding hands and writing letters to each other before they were teens. Amanda had been a part of his life for nearly as long as he had had a life. And she had been just as in love with him from that first moment as he had been with her.

CHAPTER THIRTY-TWO

Kicking off the conversation, Cal said, "Buddy, why don't you start by telling us exactly why you think there's more to all this than there appears to be."

"Gut."

"I won't let you off that easy. There's more to it than that."

"I've been a cop for a long time. I sense things. I smell things. This doesn't smell right. Harlan is my friend just like he's yours, but we're not getting the whole story. You can take that to the bank."

"You may be right," Vic interjected. "But what Cal's asking is how you're arriving at this opinion."

Buddy took a long sip from the coffee that had just been set in front of him, and then drew a deep breath before staring intently into the gray marble veneer tabletop. Without making eye contact with either of his old and trusted friends, he said, "Nothing was stolen from the Stone house."

"Maybe the guy didn't have time to steal anything," Cal added.

"You don't kick in a door at five o'clock in the morning if you're coming to burglarize. You cut out a square with a glass cutter and then unlock the window and quietly crawl through it and quietly go about the business of stealing whatever you came for. And you don't do it that late in the morning. You do it at two or three a.m. The middle of the night. Not when people just might be getting up. This guy wanted a confrontation. Not silverware or grocery money."

Neither Cal nor Vic said anything for a long moment. Then they looked at each other across the table, and the elder said to the younger, "He really is a good cop, isn't he?" When Cal nodded and smiled and agreed with him, Vic continued, "I never would have put all that together. But that's right. Why make a noise with such an entrance if you didn't want to be discovered?"

"You said earlier that you suspected one of the Drakos. How do you connect them to all this?" Cal asked.

"There's been talk. Not from Harlan, mind you. He hasn't said a word to me. Not like him not to, but he has never even hinted at anything. But everybody else in town is talking. You probably know something, Uncle Vic. You've heard the gossip. Is he gambling with them?"

Vic rubbed the expanse of his shiny forehead and grimaced when he said, "I never want to get between you boys. Never have, and don't ever want to. Especially if it might be something … oh, I don't know. Maybe something illegal."

"Like the poker games in the back of Drakos after hours every Thursday night? I know all about them," Buddy said.

"Well, there's some pretty big money passed around that table each week. Out-of-towners coming in on the train from Richmond and DC. And some local big spenders too."

"If you know all about them," Cal asked, "why hasn't somebody done something to shut them down? Breaking the law is breaking the law."

Vic and Buddy looked at each other this time, and the glance they exchanged silently asked the question of who was going to tell Cal the truth. Vic stepped up.

"Lot of important people go to those games. You've been away, but ole Nick Drakos hasn't. He's been right here, digging his heels in a little firmer every year. He's got a lot of people in town owing him."

"And you think Harlan has gambling debts to the Drakos family? That's what you think?" Cal asked Buddy directly. "You think Nick or one of his sons shot Harlan?"

"Could be."

"Have there been other incidents stemming from this secret weekly poker game?"

"Some," Buddy admitted. "Nothing as serious as somebody getting shot."

"Fights?" Cal asked.

"Yeah, fights. Even a robbery one night a couple years ago."

"Somebody robbed a poker game?"

"What easier place is there to rob?" Vic chimed in. "The money is all laid out on the table. And who's going to call the cops? Nobody that's been in the game, that's for sure."

"Did the guy get away?"

"We think he hopped a train that was leaving seconds after he ran out of the back door of the restaurant," Buddy said.

"You mean you know all about this robbery and this weekly game, and it's still going on? How come? How come you haven't closed it down?"

"Don't get riled up, Reverend," Vic said with a laugh and a hand across the table on Cal's forearm. "Mt. Jefferson's got its share of vice just like any other town, big or small."

"Yes, but if you know about it … I mean, what stops you from going in there and turning over the table and trashing the joint?" Cal was getting angry.

After another long, awkward moment, Vic spoke again. "Let me tell you exactly why, so our pal Buddy here won't have to. It'll be easier for me to say it. You see, our illustrious chief of police, William J. Westover, is a regular Thursday night customer in Drakos's back room. It would be rather unhandy for Buddy or anyone else on the force to implement the law to its fullest extent."

Cal looked wide-eyed at Buddy and asked, "Shirley Westover's daddy?"

"That would be him."

"Used to direct traffic after the football games with two flashlights?"

"Yep."

"And we used to laugh at him …"

"And we still do."

CHAPTER THIRTY-THREE

Nothing separated the Mulligans the first twenty-six years of their lives. Through high school they were even closer than in elementary years. The sports they played, the memories they made, and the people they met and knew together became the bonds that nourished the friendship into adulthood. They had planned on leaving for college together, but the health of Harlan's father put the first kink in that unfulfilled design. Harlan stayed behind to tend to the family business while Cal and Buddy went off to find their purposes in life through higher education. Even that plan didn't work out exactly as they thought it would, but in the end, all three wound up back in Mt. Jefferson. Buddy was the first to come home.

It had been preached to him by his mother from the time he walked into the door of his first-grade classroom: "You must have fifteen years of education. Don't think seven years of elementary and four of high school like so many of your friends do. You will go to college, and you will finish. I don't care what you become; I just want you to be an educated man."

She believed in him and his sister and wanted life to be as good for them as possible. On the other hand, he had heard a different message from his dad in those quiet moments of father and son.

"College is not for everyone, Buddy. I want you to go to school, but so much of that college is social. If more stress was put on the books and a little less on the parties, I'd be all for it like your mother is. But I know that's not how it is. I don't want you to disappoint her, but I also don't want you to lose who and what you are. You're a good boy, Buddy, and I don't want you spoiled."

In the long run, he pleased them both. He applied to and attended a small college in central Virginia not far from home and made grades that would have made any mother proud. He came home on all the holidays and spring breaks, helped his father at the service station, and saved every penny possible. All the time, he was staying in contact with Amanda Peers, the little girl who had now grown up to be more than just an infatuation. He knew he loved her when no other girl on campus even tempted him. And by the third year, he was ready to transfer to her campus—which he did—and he finished his business degree with honors. They came home with diplomas in their pockets and wedding bells playing in their ears and were married within a month after graduation. Both were twenty-one and ready for a life together in the hometown they loved. But finding the work they both needed presented more of a problem than they first imagined.

"Son, now that you have all that learning behind you, what are you going to do with the rest of your life?" Chub asked.

"I'm not sure, Dad. I've never been one of those who has had a burning goal or even a dream. I've always wanted to live here in Mt. Jefferson, but I have never been able to picture exactly what I want to do."

"You've got the learning for whatever you want, just like your mother wanted you to have. Not much opportunity here in this little town, though."

"Oh, I don't know. I've never wanted to live in a big city. We've got everything we need here, don't you think?"

"Me? Yeah, that's what I think. I've just always been worried about you. But if you mean it, I sure could use you here."

"What do you mean?"

"Well, the station here. Bigger than it's ever been. We made it through all the Depression years and never had to close the doors. And now we're showing good profits. More every year. And this new towing business I started while you were away is running me and Major ragged. We're getting too old to put in the hours we used to. That's where I could use you, son. You've got all the business knowledge. You take care of all the business—the books and taxes and payroll—and I'll put in a few less hours and spend some time with your mamma. What do you say?"

Buddy didn't even have to think about it. Working for and with his dad was a dream come true, and he and Amanda could stand a steady income no matter how small it might be. Within eighteen months, Chub Briggs signed over half the business to his son, and a four-by-six shingle went up over the front door: Briggs and Son Esso.

The sign went up just weeks before Christmas of 1939. Buddy and Chub would have two years, almost to the day, of prosperity and happiness in business together. And then life would become something neither one of them was expecting. And there was no way to prepare for it.

CHAPTER THIRTY-FOUR

Before Vic, Buddy, and Cal left Mulligans that afternoon, they'd decided on a strategy. Buddy noted there was no evidence that would even allow him to question one of the Drakos family members—father or sons. So Vic volunteered to see what information he might be able to gather. He offered to drop in on Nick to have coffee and a cigar as they sometimes did with each other, being neighborly restaurateurs, so he could "feel the situation out."

Cal, being a minister and Harlan's oldest friend, felt he might be able to offer some comfort and at the same time pry a little more information from Harlan. He refused to admit to Buddy that he thought Buddy had been too hard on Harlan earlier that day in the hospital room. He knew Buddy wanted him to say this, but he wasn't willing to give in just to salve Buddy's feelings. It was a friendly though certainly hard take on friendship, which only old and close pals could understand. Buddy accepted this silent and heartfelt treatment, but only from Cal. From anyone else who might give him that sideways smile, he would consider it a smirk and offer to slap it off his face.

Buddy, of the MJPD, decided and confided to his tablemates that he needed another swipe at the wife. He had to correct himself when he actually said those words and added, "I mean Darcy." He was in his police mode, and he wasn't thinking he needed to talk with Darcy again; he was thinking he needed to "take another swipe at the wife." He knew he would have to watch his manner and attitude when he went to their house. He had to constantly remind himself he was talking to an old acquaintance and the wife of a friend, not just a witness in a shooting case.

When the check came and Vic wadded it up and stuffed it in his vest pocket, they all stood up to leave for their respective destinations. They would decide later if they needed to have coffee after supper or breakfast in the morning in the same booth. Vic watched as the other two went out the door and in different directions. He said to the girl standing by the cash register, "Going up the street for a little bit. If anybody calls, I'll be back in an hour or so."

"How's Harlan?" the girl asked, giving away her eavesdropping.

Vic turned and looked at her but never answered, and then went out the door.

He was in the room alone. His eyes were closed, but he opened them when he felt someone sit down in the chair next to the bed.

"You by yourself this time?" Harlan asked.

"Yeah. How are you feeling?"

"Worse."

"Pain?"

"Pain and mad and if I could get out of this bed, me and Buddy Briggs would go round and round right there in the middle of the floor."

"Why?"

"Why? You were here. You heard it same as I did."

"Heard what? What was said that made you so mad?"

"He called me a liar, Cal. You heard him."

"Mmm. I can't say that I did. I don't recall anyone saying anybody was a liar."

"Then you weren't listening. Or you're in it with him all the way. That's probably it. I'm laid up in here, and you two are in it together, making me some kind of villain."

Cal said nothing. He turned his head slightly and looked out the window at a small hillside that butted up against the back of the hospital. It was a pleasant view for the convalescents who had to entertain themselves all day. It could also be depressing for the same patients who might long to be out there in the sunshine or to picnic on the tables that sat under the ancient pine trees. He indulged himself in these thoughts, giving his friend time to think and consider his reigning attitude. It worked because after only about forty-five seconds Harlan broke the silence and answered his own accusation.

"I'm not a villain, you know. I'm the one got shot. Looks like I'm going to be in here for a week. Maybe two. And what's going to happen to the store? Who's going to run that? You and Buddy going down there and open it up for me? You know Darcy can't do it anymore."

"Maxine?" Cal offered.

"Maxine can't even balance the cash drawer. She can sell but doesn't know a debit from a credit."

"Fritz?"

"Would you want Fritz taking your deposits to the bank and meeting with salesmen? Yeah, that's real funny."

"How *are* things at the store?"

"Meaning?"

"Meaning just that. Everything going okay? Business good?"

"Business is not great. We're selling. But there's a lot of expense. Why? Why do you ask?"

"Just concerned. You're laid up here, and I'm just wondering if you can stay open."

It was Harlan's turn to look out the window. He saw the same scene Cal had just studied, but it held none of the same meaning for him. It was just sunshine and grass, and it was making a glare in the room that hurt his eyes when it bounced off the metal bed rails. He turned his head away from it and hid behind his eyelids again.

"What do you know?" he finally asked.

"Come again?"

"Quit bulling me, Cal. What do you know? What are you getting at?"

"You tell me, old buddy. What's up?"

"The store's in trouble. I'm behind on everything. Rent. Overhead. Some personal loans. Everything coming down at once."

"Darcy know about this?"

"No. Are you going to tell her?"

"What kind of question is that?"

"I'm sorry. I'm not myself. I just got shot this morning, you know."

And they both laughed at the old Stone sense of humor.

Nothing much more was said. Cal didn't feel comfortable pushing it any further at the time. He planned to and promised to come back the next morning and knew he would have the chance to pursue the subject further without making Harlan more defensive today. Before he left, he said the prayer he had not been able to pray earlier that morning. He held Harlan's hand as he said personal things to God.

"Kind heavenly Father, we have friends in need. A friend who needs to feel Your healing hand on his body, a friend who needs to know the grace of understanding and consideration, and a friend who needs a dose of comfort and coping that comes only from You. Be in our midst and bring the warmth of Your love to our friendship. Touch this man whose hand I am holding, and give him the spirit and strength to overcome all the needs of his heart, mind, body, and soul. This simple prayer we ask in Christ's name. Amen."

When he finished, they both had tears in their eyes.

As Cal glanced out the window as he left, he noticed a father and little boy eating ice cream at one of the picnic tables. It made him want to call home again.

CHAPTER THIRTY-FIVE

Cal Vaxter never made any friends in college like the two he left behind that September morning when he boarded the train with two small suitcases in his hands and one large knot in his stomach. His mom and dad and Aunt Betty Bell and Uncle Paul and Vic Princeton were all standing on the platform to wave good-bye. Right there among them were Harlan and Buddy, full of smiles and youthful spirit. As the years passed, he remembered often that first bend when the Chesapeake and Western line took the station and all its occupants out of his sight; it was the first time he knew what homesick felt like. It was the sense that everyone else was going about their comfortable life patterns and he was the only person in the world not enjoying it with them. He was alone, and he didn't know whether to throw up or cry. For the first hundred miles he just sat silently and stared out the window at the passing blur of trees, rock hillsides, and outbuildings in backyards that only reminded him more of home and the people who mattered most to him.

He wondered what Harlan and Buddy would do that night. There had never been a time he wasn't a part of the plans. He knew Buddy would be leaving for college in two days. Harlan, of course, was already firmly in charge of his own business at the young age of seventeen. So it was time they all started thinking separately and not as a threesome. But it would take time to get used to the idea. They already knew they'd see one another at Thanksgiving and again at Christmas. And they could call on the phone and even write. But guys don't write other guys. Maybe once—maybe twice—but it was the nature of the gander not to stay in touch. For comfort's sake, gazing out that train window, he had to hope this part of their lives would not affect or change the friendship they had known nearly all their lives. He just knew it wouldn't. He would see to it.

His first few years at Duke University changed his life in dramatic ways. He got the education he was seeking, but he also experienced life in such extensive ways he questioned who he was and what his purpose in life should be. His junior year his heart took such a jolt, it changed his mind about everything he had ever pondered over and worried about. The three-year engineering student made an appointment to meet with his adviser before he even discussed it with his parents or two closest friends. He knew this was a decision he had to make by himself.

He knocked on the door of the small room in the corner of the history department.

"Come in. Come in. Come in."

"Dr. Winifred?"

"Who would you be expecting to see behind this cluttered old desk if not Dr. Winifred? That's the name on the door, isn't it, son?"

"Yes, sir, it is. And good morning to you."

Cal walked firmly toward him, extended his hand, and threw the elderly professor off his social balance. The man was tall, even sitting, and desperately thin. He had long, two-toned hair; it was easy to see he had been blond all his life and now, well into his sixth decade of life, tufts of gray were mingling with the blond. It gave him a sickly and colorless look about his face. He frowned as he shook Cal's hand and left him standing for too long just to get a look at him and show him who was in charge. He finally took his gaze off the young student and said, "Sit. Move those books. Sit."

Cal moved a heavy stack of six or seven books to the floor and then sat in a straight chair that wobbled and threatened to spill him with every shifting of his weight. He was patient while the old man in front of him shuffled paper and files until he finally settled on one and opened it. He studied it for what seemed like three or four minutes before speaking.

"James Calvin Vaxter. Third year, civil engineering. Mmm. What do you want to build, James? Bridges? Buildings? Pipe dreams?"

"Well, actually, sir, that's what I came to speak to you about."

"It says here, you're from Virginia. Mt. Jefferson. I've heard of that. Think I've been through there a time or two. There's a man from there ... he's a pro golfer ... what is his name?"

"Vic Princeton. That's his hometown."

"Yeah, that's right. Princeton. I love golf. Can't play it all that well. Never could. Let's see now, what's on your mind today, James?"

"Well, sir, it's really Cal. I don't go by James. But I think I want to change my major."

"You think you do."

"I know I do."

"You're in engineering now. What are you looking at changing to?"

"I want to go into the ministry."

Dr. Winifred looked at Cal a long, long time before speaking another word. It was not so much disbelief on his face and in his eyes as it was distrust. When he finally decided to continue the conversation, there was more cynicism in his voice than ever.

"Do you know what you're saying, son? You came here two and a half years ago with engineering in mind. That's a tangible, material, solid thing. Bridges and houses and canals and ... and now you want to go to the very opposite and seek something that is not tangible or material or solid at all. That's a big jump, James."

"I know, sir. I've thought about it and prayed about it, and I know for sure this is what I want to do."

"Some big road-to-Damascus experience you've had that changed your mind?"

"Maybe."

"Maybe it changed your mind, or maybe you don't want to talk about it?"

"I came to talk about the process of changing my major. Not really to talk about why."

"You've got a little bit of an edge to your tone, don't you. James? You don't like me interrogating you, do you?"

"I have nothing to hide if that's what you mean."

"Oh, come on, boy. We all have something to hide. And those who say they don't, usually have the most."

There was uneasy silence again in the room until the old professor broke it.

"So, what do you say?"

"I'm sorry, sir. I didn't realize what you said last required an answer."

"James Calvin Vaxter, why do you want to become a preacher? Does dressing up every Sunday morning in a blue suit and a white shirt and performing in front of people from the pulpit appeal to you?"

"Certainly."

"And do you think you'd like marrying men and women and sending them off on a lifetime of bliss? Think you can do that?"

"I think I could."

"And does it appeal to you to counsel lost souls who don't want to hear what you say and will ignore the good advice you offer them? Do you want to visit jails and prisons and hear heart-wrenching stories where you can't discern the truth from the con? Do you relish walking into sickrooms and hospitals and holding the hands of the hopeless and praying for the dying even when you know there's not a chance in heaven or hell for their recovery? And do you look forward to breaking the news to families who will scream and cry at the messenger and leave you as emotionally drained as they are themselves? Are you prepared to preside over more funerals than you will baptisms? Are you ready to be a referee between church members no matter how petty the problem and see children abused and the elderly forsaken and know that even though you'd give your very heart to make a difference, you probably won't? No matter how hard you try and how much you yourself grieve over it? Is this what you want out of life?"

"Dr. Winifred, you don't paint a very pretty picture. But if you think you're listing things I haven't thought of, then you must think I have an extremely shallow soul. This is not a whim. This is what I want."

"Two and a half years ago you wanted to be a civil engineer. How do you know two and a half years from now you won't want to change again?"

"Because the decision then was mine. This one is God's."

Dr. Alvin Winifred stacked papers on his desk, straightened his blotter and his pens, and reached in his top left-hand drawer and took out a form. He signed it and handed it over the desktop. "I'm just a lowly little history teacher who doesn't know much about anything except the dates of battles and the signings of treaties and such things as that. But I've lived a few years longer than you, and I've learned not to always trust my instincts. Instincts are sometimes just excuses for the lack of preparedness. Fill this out, and turn it in to the administrative office."

"Thank you, sir. I appreciate your help, although I sense you don't approve."

Winifred smiled. "You could be wrong, you know."

"Yes, sir. And I hope I am."

As Cal crossed the room and opened the door, he didn't look back at the professor/adviser until the old man spoke.

"You are wrong in thinking I don't approve. I'm an elder in the First Presbyterian Church here in Durham. I'll pray for you. Godspeed and good luck, Cal."

CHAPTER THIRTY-SIX

The changes came easy for Cal, and when college ended in the spring of '37, he went immediately into Duke Divinity School. He was led by his passion to learn and by his dedication to the faith in which he was reared. He thought of Dr. Alvin Winifred many times over the next years of study and was taken by the summary of his chosen profession that the elder professor had compacted into a dramatic soliloquy in his tiny office. But he was also amused at all the negative components the man had included without touching on any of the positives. And that's what Cal Vaxter saw with each passing day. The good he could do. The fulfillment he felt in doing it. And the knowledge he gained with each subject and class. He loved every minute of hard work that went into his degree. He even looked forward to the responsibility that would go with the commitment. He was sure he could handle it. And, yes, he wanted to minister to the people. He wanted to make a difference, no matter how small the scale. Ever since his heart had been touched that special night, he had been changed. And he had talked to no one about it. To do so at that point would be to denigrate the sanctity of the experience. Someday he would be able to put it all into words, but now he would just have to answer all the questions from his family and friends—"What made you want to go into the ministry? You're the last one I would ever have thought would do that"—with a smile and knowing headshake. "Just something I felt led to do" was as far as he was willing to go.

Durham had become like a second home. He loved the feel of the town even though it was quite a bit bigger than Mt. Jefferson. But it didn't take him long to adjust and feel like he belonged. It became even easier when he met a town girl at a local restaurant one fall evening when he was eating by himself.

"Excuse me. Could I borrow your saltshaker? Nothing will come out of mine."

Cal looked up from the book he was reading: The Pilgrim's Regress *by C. S. Lewis. He focused for a second on the girl in the booth next to his table and said, "Sure," and handed her the requested shaker.*

Then he added, "They get damp and clog up."

"You must be a science student. You talk like you know something about the atmosphere." She laughed.

"No. Just that I've filled up about a million of those little devils in my life. I worked in a restaurant when I was growing up."

"Really? You a chef or something?"

"Hardly. I bused tables and waited and swept up. Everything except cooking. But I do know how to keep that salt from going solid on you. Put a few grains of rice in there, and it will flow like water."

"Good to know." She smiled. "I'll just pull my bag of white rice out of my purse and go table to table and fix them all."

They laughed.

"You'll make somebody a good wife," she teased.

"I can't tell if that's sarcasm or a come-on."

"Suit yourself."

At this point, Cal took a closer look and liked what he saw. She had short dark hair that curled around a heart-shaped face and green eyes that seemed to stop just short of looking into his brain.

"You waiting on someone?" he asked.

"Not particularly."

"Me either. You're welcome to join me, if you like," he invited.

"That doesn't seem quite right. Why don't you join me?"

Cal picked up his iced tea and moved to the booth with the pretty girl with the viridescent eyes.

"What're you reading?"

"C. S. Lewis. You familiar with him?"

"Can't say I am. I don't read much. No time for it."

"Well, just what do you do that would keep you so busy you don't have time to read an occasional book?"

"I work. In an office. A small office. So I stay pretty busy all day long and most nights."

"A secretary?"

"I resent that, thank you very much."

"Oh, excuse me. What did I say wrong?"

"I'm a CPA. Official and licensed."

"Well, now. I'm impressed. What led a pretty young lady like you into the world of correctional finance?"

"That's a smart-aleck way of putting it."

"Well, it's true, isn't it? You keep books for people who can't keep them for themselves. And you advise and correct their mistakes."

"It's a little more than that, and you make it sound so much less."

"Maybe we're starting off on the wrong foot here. I was just having fun with you because you looked so friendly. Let's start fresh. What's your name, pretty young lady?"

"My name is Ellie. I work at Harnott Associates. I'm a certified public accountant. I'm single and have Saturdays and Sundays off. I like fishing and tennis. I don't dance, and I hate fried chicken. I was born in Louisville, went to school at Duke, and got this job my senior year and have decided to stay here until I find something I like better. Now, what about you, near-handsome young man?"

She made Cal laugh again and not for the last time. He loved her edgy personality and the sharp, biting words that came out of her timid-looking little mouth. She was an enigma of contradictions, and he was pretty sure he had fallen in love with her before the salad came.

CHAPTER THIRTY-SEVEN

Christina Melito Drakos was nearly six feet tall. Her hair was a perfect mix of natural gray and original black. She carried her three score and three years with such grace, women half her age paled in the presence of her beauty. She smiled when she saw Vic open the front door and walked to him and hugged him with equal parts sincere greeting and pure affection.

"How's the love of my life?" he asked softly.

"Still the love of your life. Where have you been keeping yourself?"

"Laboring day and night just like you."

"Every day, we're less than two blocks from each other, and I see you, what, three, four times a year?"

"You're forgetting, my love—you have a husband. And speaking of such, where is the royal Nick?"

"In the back. If he sees you out here, he'll be out. And pretty quick, too."

The customers dining in the dimly lit setting paid no attention to the slick-haired man in the gray suit and dark tie as he came through the swinging doors from the kitchen and breezed past their tables. They had seen him do it many times in pursuit of an arriving customer. He walked to the man and woman standing near the front door and reached out his hand.

"Hello, Prince."

"Nick." Vic shook his hand.

"Did you finally stop in to get a decent meal for a change?"

"Don't have the time. But I will take a decent cup of coffee. Providing you know how to make one."

Nick's guffaw gave way for Christina's exit, and the two men walked to and sat at the most private table near the back. Nick sat so he could still see the front door. Vic understood. Had they been down the street, Nick would have allowed him the same courtesy.

"You haven't come to tell me you want me to buy you out, have you?" Nick said through a half grin.

"No, no. Why would you think that?"

"Just wishful thinking. And you're getting closer to that retirement age all the time. Maybe past it."

"I'm no older than you are, Nick."

"Well, if you've come to borrow money, I'm your man."

"Not that either. Did you hear about Harlan Stone this morning?"

"Yeah. Yeah, I did. What a shame. Said somebody just walked in his house and let him have it."

"The police have ideas about who it was."

"Really? Suspects already?"

"Ideas. And I was wondering if you could help. You got any thoughts on who might have it in for the boy? Who he might be in debt to or indebted to?"

Nick Drakos put all his attention on tearing off half of the tinfoil top from his fresh pack of Lucky Strikes. He patted one out and tossed the rest across the table to Vic. He took his time lighting up with a gold-encrusted lighter, and after exhaling the first deep drag, he looked up at the man with his back to the door.

"When did you go to work for the local police, Prince?"

"Just concerned for the boy, Nick."

"Yeah, you took those little punks under your wing when they were kids, didn't you? One turned out to be a cop. One a preacher. And one a jeweler."

Nick laughed too big and too long at the nonjoke he had made.

"Now, I'll let you decide which one was more apt to get into trouble," Nick said. "Lots of money in those baubles he wholesales and retails up there in that little goldmine of his. You mother-henned those boys, and two out of three—that's not bad, Prince. So don't waste your time fretting over the jeweler."

Nick laughed again while Vic stared him down.

"Has he been in the games, Nick?"

"Games?"

"Who does he owe?"

"You're going to have to be more specific with me, old friend of mine. Say what you mean."

"Who does Harlan owe money to? Local boys or the out-of-towners?"

"I'm not a banker, Prince. I run a restaurant just like you do."

"Yeah, but you run it from the back room with the shades down on Thursday nights. Don't play dumb with me, Nick. The boy has been shot, and there could be a lot of people in this town hurt if it came from one of those games."

"Harlan Stone doesn't owe me a dime. Is that what you want to hear?"

"I want to hear the truth."

"Well, you just did. And you've heard all there is to hear about it. I have a party of thirty coming in here for some kind of school reunion in about twenty minutes. So we're going to have to break up this little get-together. Sure nice of you stop in and say hi, Prince. Come back anytime. Always good to see you."

Vic stood and paused to say something but wasn't sure he could control his temper long enough to get it out. And he didn't want to damage anything for Buddy's investigation. As he went to the front door, he caught Christina's eye from where she stood by the register. But he didn't react to her because he could still feel Nick's eyes piercing him in the back.

CHAPTER THIRTY-EIGHT

Darcy Brennaman got a job teaching grade school. It's what she had dreamed of ever since she was barely five years old, lining up her rag dolls and china dolls and her collie, Lady, on the front porch and, with a ruler in her hand, teaching them the "A-B-C" song, running through the alphabet musically and ending with "next time sing along with me." Sitting at her desk in front of real children now, she had to smile as she remembered teaching that old 1835 children's song to her make-believe subjects. Here she was now with real first graders, and they actually sang it back to her. This was just one of her dreams that was coming true.

The other one would be picking her up after school and taking her to dinner in Richmond. Just the two of them on a long, romantic Friday evening. She had confided to her closest girlfriends that she felt sure she had conquered Mt. Jefferson's most renowned Romeo and bachelor. When they would set the date had become just a matter of assumption. She would like it in the spring of the coming year. And with nearly two whole years of dating and getting to know one another behind them, the "Spring of '39" had a nice matrimonial ring to it. She and Harlan would talk about it at dinner. It was a long road trip down and back to the capital city, so she would feel him out and make the proposal official.

"A penny for your thoughts," Darcy said.

"That should be some easy money. I'm just concentrating on this highway. This is the most boring stretch of road I've ever driven. Just miles and miles of straight up-and-down road for as far as you can see."

"You want the radio on?"

"Only if you do."

She quickly spun the dial and, getting nothing but static and high whistles and an occasional news report, clicked it off for the lack of decent music. She wanted to talk anyway.

"You thought any more about what we talked about the other night?" she asked.

"What did we talk about? Going to the movies, or you working part time for me at the store over Christmas?"

"Neither, silly. You know what I'm talking about."

"Getting married. That wouldn't be it, now would it?"

"You're so smart, Mr. Stone. You should really be on one of those radio quiz shows."

"No doubt. I've got all the answers. You just throw me the questions."

"Okay. When?"

"Right now. I'm ready."

"No. That was *the question. When? When are we going to get married?"*

Harlan paused just a little too long to satisfy Darcy's hunger for the subject. She stared out the windshield, watching the tall trees and hillsides whiz past, but the silence in the car was getting louder by the second. Finally she looked at Harlan, and he was staring back at her. At first she was startled at his gaze but then became frightened at how long he held her eyes with his.

"Watch the road, Harlan! Or you're going to kill us both!"

She grabbed for the wheel, but he pulled it back to the center of the lane just before she had a chance to grip it with both hands. She wound up nearly sitting on his lap as he jerked the steering wheel and threw her toward him. With his right hand he grabbed her around the shoulders and held her tight, their faces a mere two inches from one another.

"Darcy Brennaman. Can you hear me? Can you?"

"Yes." She was not frightened but a little taken back at this unexpected reaction to her original question.

"I love you. With all my heart and soul. Wasn't it me who proposed to you eighteen months ago on the front steps of your house at midnight in the moonlight?"

"Yes."

"And what did you tell me?"

"That I wasn't ready to take that step and that I ... "

"And that you wanted to think about it. And wasn't it me who asked you again six months later in the back booth of Mulligans while we cut your birthday cake?"

"It was. And ... "

"And you said no again. Some guys' egos can't take that many rejections. Some guys would be gone by now and never ask again. And the other night when we talked about marriage in your driveway with the heater running full blast, I didn't propose again, did I?"

"No, you didn't."

"You know why? Because I'm not going to be turned down again. When I ask again, it's going to be yes. Do you understand?"

"Yes, Mr. Stone, I do. And it will be."

Harlan released his playful grip on her and looked into the face that had only grown lovelier since the post-office episode. He smiled his full-charm smile and showed her all his teeth. That was the smile he saved for all the beauties when he wanted to make his biggest impression. But this time he wasn't conscious of even doing it. This time it just came natural.

"I have never asked anyone else to marry me, Darcy. No one. So one more time. Will you marry me?"

"Yes, yes, yes."

"How is this time different from the other two times you said no?"

"Well, I never really said no. I just said I wasn't ready, which was kind of a lie. Oh, I was ready. Boy, was I ready! I was just not sure you were."

"And you're sure now that I am?"

"I think so. All we have to decide is when and where."

"I'll leave all that up to you. The sooner the better."

"Oh, I can't believe it. Since I was a little girl, I have dreamed of a big church wedding!"

"Really?"

"What?"

"Nothing. I was just thinking … let's make it a party. Get a judge to do the honors and have the whole thing at the country club. But I guess we could have the actual wedding at a church if you really want to."

There was silence again as Darcy remembered the conversation she and her daddy had had that evening on the porch. She had ended it with a promise that she would bring Harlan to church with her, and yet, after two years of courtship, she hadn't been able to fulfill that promise. Her

dad didn't mention it, and she knew he never would. But a country club
wedding. This might not be as easy to explain away.

"What's wrong? You didn't go to sleep over there, did you? What do
you think?"

"I'm thinking we have a lot to come to terms with, Harlan. We've got
a lot of things to work out."

"I didn't say something wrong, did I? You finally say yes, and then I
say something wrong."

CHAPTER THIRTY-NINE

Time and circumstance can change the best-laid plans, and the meeting Vic, Buddy, and Cal had intended that evening after their respective interviews fell prey to these very ingredients. Buddy's meeting with Darcy, where he had hoped to ask harder questions than the softballs he threw her earlier that day, couldn't be coordinated with her hospital visits. Then the station required Buddy's presence on other matters in the late afternoon, so Darcy had agreed for him to stop by the house the next morning before she went back to spend the day at Harlan's bedside. That morning, Buddy knocked at the same back door, where the uniformed policeman had been posted all day yesterday. This morning, everything looked to be back to normal, and he could hear Darcy in the kitchen through the open windows.

"Coming."

Buddy waited with his back to the screen and petted their golden retriever, Chipper, on the head as the dog frisked about his feet.

"Come in, Buddy," Darcy said. "I was just fixing some coffee."

"I'll take you up on that. Does he come in or out?"

"Oh, let him in. He has the run of the house." Then she said directly to the dog, "Go lay down, boy." Chipper found his corner on the cool kitchen tile.

"You like it black best, I recall."

"Yeah, that's fine," Buddy said. "You heard from Harlan this morning?"

"Yes. He had a pretty rough night. He's in a lot of pain and very doped up. A nurse said the pain was normal and may get worse over the next couple of days before it gets better. And he's still mad at you."

"Even through the pain and the dope, he still found the strength to dump on me?"

"I think you hurt him yesterday, Buddy. You were pretty harsh with him, considering the shape he was in."

"Maybe so. And you thought I was too harsh with you, too?"

"Not really, although I didn't appreciate you making me leave the room while you three guys talked. There was no sense in that, and yes, that made me pretty mad."

"Sorry, Darcy. That's the last thing I wanted to do. But if you were mad yesterday, you'll probably kick me out of here today, because I'm not through."

"You've still got more questions?"

"Let's start all over again."

"No, Buddy. I'm not doing that. I told you all I know. Somebody broke in my home yesterday morning and shot my husband, and I am very upset. And that's all I know to tell you, and I don't appreciate being treated like a criminal."

"And I don't appreciate being treated like an outsider. I have a job to do, and please don't tell me what you will and won't do. If you

want the same thing I want, you'll answer any question I ask. My one
and only goal is to find out who was in here yesterday morning, and
you're the only person right now that can help me with that. So calm
down. There is no reason for you to make an enemy out of me. Let's
get on the same side here. Okay?"

"Okay." She sat down at the Early American kitchen table and
put sugar in her cup. Buddy followed suit.

"Tell me anything and everything you can to describe this
person. His height, hair color, skin color, his clothes, his hands, any
odor he may have carried. Did he move like he was twenty or fifty?
Were his shoes dirty or shined? Was his voice old, young, high, low?
Just anything at all." Buddy waited for her answer.

"His clothes were dark. Black, I think. And he was completely
covered up. He had that horrible mask on, and I couldn't see any
skin. His gloves were black just like his clothes, and he moved kind
of quick-like."

"He had on gloves?"

"Yes. Leather gloves, I think."

"You didn't mention the gloves yesterday."

"I didn't? I was so upset yesterday."

"How about his skin?"

"I don't know about his skin."

"Yesterday you said he was white but with a dark complexion."

"I did? Maybe so then. I'm not real clear on that."

"You don't know if he wore gloves or if you saw his skin."

"Buddy, what are you trying to do to me?" she screamed with
tears forming in her eyes. "I don't know. Can't you just accept that I
was upset and scared, and I just don't know?"

"I'm trying to help you remember."

"No, you're not. You're trying to trip me up for some reason. You didn't believe Harlan yesterday at the hospital, and you don't believe me now. What do you want from us?"

"I want the truth. Darcy, I think you know who stood in this very kitchen and drew a gun and shot your husband just a little over twenty-four hours ago. I don't think he came to rob you, and I think you could put me on the right track right this very minute if only you would."

Darcy got up and poured the coffee left in the cup from her everyday dishes into the sink. She went back to the table and picked up Buddy's cup and said, "Are you through with this?"

When he nodded, she said, "Then you're through here."

Buddy sat at the table, not out of defiance, but trying to make sense of what his next move should be in order to get the optimum results from the interview. If it were all business, he knew what he'd do. But it wasn't, and that was the thing tying his hands at every turn.

Darcy walked around his chair and disappeared through the dining room. He heard her go up the steps and, in a few seconds more, heard the bedroom door slam. Chipper walked over and laid his chin on Buddy's knee, and after rubbing the old dog's head for a few moments, Buddy got up and went out the back door into the sunlight.

Closing the screen door behind him, he heard the phone ring inside the house. It stopped after the second ring, so he figured Darcy had gotten it. He walked to his police cruiser and sat down on the already hot seat cushion and started the engine. As he was about to back up to turn the car around, he heard Darcy's voice through the open window.

"Buddy! Buddy!"

He switched the engine off, got out of the car, and looked up to a window on the back of the house. Darcy was leaning out.

"It's Maxine on the phone. Maxine from the store. I think you might want to talk to her."

Darcy met him as he was coming back through the dining room and pointed to a telephone on a chair in the hallway near the front door. She stood over him, nervously twisting her ring and watch while he picked up the phone and talked to Maxine.

"Hello."

"Buddy, this Maxine at Stone's. I don't know if it means anything or not, but I thought Darcy should know, and she felt you should know."

"What's up?"

"I can't find Fritz."

"What do you mean you can't find him?"

"He hasn't come in to work. He didn't come in all day yesterday, and now he's not here this morning, and I don't know quite what to do."

"Does he miss work very often?"

"Never. He's never even been late in thirty-five years."

"What about yesterday? Why didn't you check it out yesterday?"

"Well, I did. After I heard about Harlan and got over the shock of it myself, I tried to find him. I thought maybe he was home by himself and maybe he was upset too. He doesn't have a telephone, but I called his landlady and she knocked on his door and couldn't raise him."

"Has she gone in his apartment or just knocked on the door?"

"Well, this morning I had her go in. And it's not really an apartment. It's just a room he's always rented from Agnes Coraday. You know out there on West Beverley Street?"

"Yeah, I know where it is. What did she find?"

"Nothing. He's not there. And I guess that means he wasn't there yesterday either. It's just not like him, and I worry that something might have happened to him."

"I'll go out there and look and see if I can pick up on anything. Thanks for calling, Maxine."

"And thank you for checking on him. And Buddy—how's Darcy doing? Is she holding up okay? I know she can be a little high strung and take things to the extreme sometimes."

"Then considering all that, Maxine, I'd say she's doing just fine."

"Thank you, Buddy. And call me if you find out something."

They said good-bye, and as Buddy put the phone back in its cradle, he saw Darcy standing on the second step of the staircase, seemingly not knowing whether to ascend or descend.

"Where do you think he is?" she asked.

"I have no idea."

"Do you think it means anything?"

"I have no idea."

And good ole Chipper saw Buddy to the door again.

CHAPTER FORTY

By the "Spring of '39," plans had been made, as well as a few compromises. Leading up to the day, Darcy and Harlan spent nearly every evening together, and most of them ended in arguments. If they were going to the movies, they were usually late because they couldn't come to an agreement on a comedy or a drama, Cary Grant or Spencer Tracy. If they were going to eat, they fell out over whether they wanted to get a sit-down dinner or grab a quick sandwich at a café. They even disagreed on what brand of gasoline to use in their cars; what radio shows they'd listen to; what friends they would go to dances with—and Amanda and Buddy remembered, and still laughed about, the night Harlan and Darcy yelled feverishly at each other over which side they were going to sit on at a high school football game. They both held out for their home schools, and Amanda wound up sitting with Darcy in the bleachers while Buddy stood on the opposite sideline with Harlan and ate hot dogs and peanuts.

But mostly they just argued about the wedding. Harlan wanted to keep it simple and do it soon. Darcy wanted it big and fairy-tale–like and wanted plenty of time to plan it. He wanted it to be a suit-and-tie occasion while she demanded a formal affair; the veiled gown and train with equal numbers of bridesmaids and groomsmen. He contended they should save the money for the honeymoon while she maintained that her daddy and mother were paying for it so it should be no skin off his hide how much it cost. He wanted to invite no more than fifty people, and she wanted invitations for at least two hundred and fifty since her family was bigger than his and fifty wouldn't begin to accommodate her clan. And Harlan was still holding out for the country club location. When he had to give in on the number of guests, he used that to bolster his case that the club room would hold so many more than the local Presbyterian church.

"But a country club is for dances. People go there to get drunk and hang on other people's wives. It is no place for a wedding," Darcy argued.

"A wedding is a wedding no matter where you have it. You come away just as married if you have it in a barn or in the middle of a carnival."

"Yes, maybe that's what we'll do. We'll get on the Ferris wheel and let the minister go around with us and take our vows."

"Okay by me. And that's something else. We don't need a minister. It can be a justice of the peace or a judge. It doesn't have to be a preacher."

"I am not getting married by some lawyer in a black robe. It will be a minister who marries me, or there will be no wedding."

"Well, now that is an option worth considering. That just might be the way to go, now that I think about it."

One of them would go out the door and slam it behind them. And a few days later, history would repeat itself with variations on the dialogue and embellishments on the details.

But in the end, concessions were traded and modifications were made and not only a date (April 29th), but a place (the Mt. Jefferson Country Club) and a presiding official (the Reverend Parker Tate of the Faith Presbyterian Church) were decided on even if not agreed upon. Darcy cried over the country club and Harlan pouted over Reverend Tate, but in the end the "Spring of '39" came and went, not without its quandaries and a few vexing moments—but for all concerned, they left the grounds as a happy bride and groom.

The one dark element was H. V. Stone's health. He had been in and out of the hospital for years after his initial stroke and heart attack. He had done little to take proper care of himself, and in his final years he spent more and more time in bed than he did even in the back room of Stone's. His health had taken a toll on Esther's, and she looked older, more tired, and even sicker than he did. But come the week of their only child's wedding, Esther vowed she wouldn't let anything prevent her from being there. And she didn't. Even H. V.'s return to the hospital the night before the wedding rehearsal didn't detain her.

Harlan was worried about his dad, and if it hadn't been for Cal coming home from seminary to be at the wedding and Buddy's daily support, he might not have been able to see it through. His dad was to be his best man and his two best friends his ushers. But the call from his mother telling him about H. V.'s latest setback sent him speeding for Lenity General Hospital to be at his dad's side.

"You all right, Dad?"

"I'm all right. I may not get out of here to get to that wedding of yours, but don't let that spoil anything."

"We'll postpone it till you're strong enough to come."

"No, we won't, son. We won't do any such thing. This is not my *wedding. This is yours and Darcy's."*

"I don't care. I'm not standing up there without you. We'll wait till you get out."

"Listen to me, Harlan. Don't you know anything about women? All those girls you ran with all those years, and you still don't know anything about them? You don't postpone a woman's wedding day. You honor it. She's your wife, or going to be in about forty-eight hours. So you do what's right by her. Me being there isn't going to matter a hoot in a hollow. It's about you and her. Now get your butt over there and get on with that wedding, and I don't want to hear anymore about it. And tell Darcy to come see me. I want to kiss the bride."

H. V. Stone spent his only son's wedding day in room 326 in Mt. Jefferson's only hospital. His absence was bigger than all the others' attendance and nearly stole the show from the bride's gown and glory.

It was a four o'clock wedding, and by seven thirty the reception was in full swing. The Rhythm Kings, a small dance band from Roanoke, was providing the music that had the ballroom floor full and the party pitched to a high fever. No one seemed to notice when one participant sneaked out the side door with a small package in hand. In this crowd it would be easy for anyone to go missing for a few minutes to run an important errand.

H. V. was listening to the Washington Senators ballgame on the radio. His eyes were closed, and his mind was going back and forth from childhood memories of Harlan to what was happening on the field. When he was thinking about the game, he was wondering if this might be the year Bucky Harris would bring the team back from their doldrums. Bucky had been the best second baseman in baseball, but he was proving to be only a mediocre manager. And when H. V. was thinking of Harlan, he was wondering if Harlan would be as good a husband as he had been a son. The boy had been running the family business since seventeen years of age and doing a bang-up job. H. V.'s own health had robbed the lad of his education, but he had never heard Harlan complain about anything he might have missed out on in life. His son was a man before he ever had the chance to be a complete teenager, and H. V. only hoped Harlan would continue to be the man his family would need him to be. Lying alone in a hospital bed with pain as a constant companion, H. V. sensed the family just might need his son to be that man any day now.

That's when he felt someone in the room. Before he could open his eyes, he heard a voice say, "I thought I'd bring the party to you. Even a man in bed can eat a piece of wedding cake and drink a little punch."

Chapter Forty-One

"Mrs. Coraday? I'm Lieutenant Briggs with the Mt. Jefferson Police."

"Yes, come in. Maxine said you might come by."

"When was the last time you saw Fritz?"

"Oh, I couldn't say, Mr. Briggs. I never see Fritz. I mean, it may have been months since I've laid eyes on him. But that doesn't mean anything. Not anything at all because you see, I hardly ever see him at all."

"Does he have his own entrance to his room?"

"Oh, yes sir. He comes in that door around there. Would you like to look through his room?"

"Yes, I would."

Buddy found nothing suspicious. What he did find was rather neat, clean, and sparse living quarters confined to one room with a shared bath down the hallway. There were only a few clothes hanging in the small closet. Besides the bed, the only furniture was a nightstand with a radio and soiled doily and an overstuffed easy chair with a footstool that neither matched nor coordinated. A tall, skinny bookcase stood in one corner and held a few tattered hardbacks written in a foreign language. Buddy wasn't sure, but thought it was one of the Latin languages. Knowing Fritz's nationality might have helped him in determining which. The room smelled of the same chicken broth Fritz always smelled of but appeared spotless. There was no hint of anything that could explain the old man's absence from work.

Once back in his car, Buddy took on the duty of every police officer involved in a case. He had to evaluate all the information at hand and ask himself what the next logical move was. Mulling over everything he had gathered, learned, or assumed, he felt in his bones that it was time to drop in to the hospital for another visit. It was almost 10:00 a.m. He knew this meant he might run into Darcy again but couldn't let that deter him from seeing Harlan.

The drive from the west end of Beverley Street to the hospital took him through the center of town, and while sitting at a red light, he heard someone call his name.

"Where you heading on such a sunny summer morning, and why the long face?" Vic Princeton asked as he peered into Buddy's passenger-side window.

"Uncle Vic. Didn't know I was looking so sour. But it's already been a rough morning. Have you talked to Cal?"

"No, I haven't. We still getting together sometime today to compare notes?"

"For sure. I'll stop by or call you about lunchtime."

"Good boy. Where you going now?"

"To see Harlan. Not to question him. Just to visit."

"So am I. I was just walking down the street to get my car."

"Ride with me. I'll bring you back, and we'll call Cal when we get through."

"Sounds like a winner." Vic jumped in the police car beside Buddy as the light turned green.

Buddy and Vic were walking through the front lobby and heading for the elevator when they spotted a man in a tie and shirtsleeves practically running toward them in an effort to cut them off.

"Excuse me. Excuse me, please," he called.

Both men stopped short and looked at the man, who wore a worried and urgent expression.

"I'm sorry to stop you, but aren't you with the police department?"

"Yes, I am," Buddy answered.

"We have a little problem here. Could I see you in my office, if you don't mind?"

Buddy followed the tall, thin man and motioned for Vic to come with him. All three walked back through the lobby to a suite of offices located behind the reception desk. When they had entered and closed the door, the man turned abruptly in the center of the room and began talking without offering anyone a seat or any further greeting.

"I'm Arlo Stanley. I'm the hospital administrator here."

"I know who you are, Mr. Stanley. I'm Lieutenant Briggs. This is Vic Princeton. What can I do for you?"

"Mr. Princeton. How do you do? We have a problem with a most unusual man. Since yesterday morning, we have a man who has taken up residence in that little alcove in the front lobby and won't leave even when we close the front doors at eight p.m. He slept here all night last night, and when he was asked to leave, he became belligerent and refused to go."

"Did you call the police?"

"No. I wasn't here, but I think he scared the staff, so they didn't know what to do. When I got here early this morning I tried to reason with him and remove him, but he won't budge."

"Where is he now?"

"In the bathroom. He has been right outside this door in a corner chair, but he went to the bathroom just before you two walked in."

"Is he causing a disturbance?"

"No, Lieutenant, he's just sitting there. But we can't have that. This is not a hotel. It's a hospital, and you can't just camp out in the lobby."

"Let's go see if he's back out here," Buddy said as he turned for the door.

"Lieutenant, please be careful. The man might be dangerous, and I'm responsible for the people in that lobby," Arlo Stanley said curtly.

"I understand, Mr. Stanley. So am I."

The man in question had resumed his position in a chair in the corner of the waiting room. He was not reading a magazine or talking to anyone sitting close to him. He was simply staring straight ahead at nothing and no one in particular.

"Good morning, Fritz. I've been looking for you," Buddy said quietly.

"I be right here."

"Did you come to see Harlan?"

"No."

"Then why are you here?"

"I can't be here?"

"Sure, you can be here. But you can't stay here. Can't sleep here all night. Why would you want to?"

Fritz looked up and saw Vic standing behind Buddy and glared at him instead of answering the question. The stare over his shoulder went on so long that Buddy turned to look at Vic and then back at Fritz.

"That's Vic Princeton. You know him, don't you?" Buddy asked.

"I know him," Fritz replied

"We're here to see Harlan. Would you like to go up with us and visit with him for a minute?"

"No. I stay right here."

"You can't stay right here, Fritz," Buddy said firmly. "You have to go up and visit someone, or you have to leave. I'll be glad to give you a ride home."

"Not necessary. I'm going nowhere," Fritz said defiantly.

"What's the purpose for you being here if you're not going up to see him?"

"I'm sitting vigilance."

Buddy walked away a few steps and was followed by Vic and Arlo Stanley. Buddy said in low tones, only for their ears and in particular to Vic, "Do you know what's going on?"

"Yeah," Vic said in a whisper. "He's here to protect Harlan from his attacker. He's a weird old duck. He's not apt to leave peacefully. And I can't help with him. He hasn't talked to me for thirty years. He doesn't like me. You may have to take him out of here physically."

"I don't want to do that." Buddy thought for a moment and then directed his thoughts to Arlo. "Can we use your office and your phone for a few minutes?"

"Sure. Anything you need."

Buddy walked back to Fritz and whispered something in his ear. Fritz sat for a moment, stone-faced as ever, and then got up slowly and followed Buddy into the administrator's office with Vic and Arlo Stanley close behind.

Chapter Forty-Two

As the solitude of H. V. Stone's refuge was broken, he opened his eyes to welcome his visitor. But he knew even before he held him in his sights whose voice it was. And it made him smile from way down inside.

"Well, I'll be. Little Cal Vaxter. How in the world are you, son?"

"I'm here to see how you are."

"In the hospital, flat on my back. How do you think I am?"

"That doesn't automatically rule out cake and icing does it?"

"If my doctor was here, it would. But who's going to tell?"

They hugged. Cal's lifelong next-door neighbor and H. V.'s son's life-long friend. Then Cal set the cake on a napkin, put it on the bedside tray, and carefully pulled a paper cup of punch from the bag in his hand. H. V. immediately sat up as if dessert was a prescribed medicine.

"Turn that radio down some," H. V. barked. "I can listen to that anytime. I want to hear about you. You a preacher yet?"

"Still in school. I should graduate from seminary next summer."

"Then you'll get your license and be ready for business."

"Yeah"—Cal laughed—"get my license."

"Well, it's like any other business, is it not? You can't turn a buck until you have the license on your wall. I have to get one every January."

Cal got comfortable in the chair by the bed while H. V. started in on the cake.

"How was the wedding?" H. V. asked with his mouth full.

"All done. You now officially have a daughter."

"Good. I like that girl. How about you? You got a girl?"

"As a matter of fact, I do. Met her in Durham. She's from Kentucky."

"You going to marry her?"

"Probably. But not for another fourteen months. I want school completely behind me before I take on anything else."

"Good thinking, son. And good cake, too."

They both laughed.

"How did Harlan finally handle that best man thing? Did he kick you up from an usher? He said he might do that."

"No. Buddy and I were the ushers along with two of Darcy's cousins. I don't know their names."

"Aw. I thought he said you were going to stand in for me in the best-man spot. Who did it, then?"

"Uncle Vic."

"Really?"

"What's wrong? Does that bother you?"

"A little. He always was vying for my position with Harlan. And yours, too, with your dad and Chub Briggs. I never said much, but it ate at me. I think Harlan felt closer to Vic a lot of times than he did me. You'll understand that when you have kids. You don't want anybody getting between you and your son."

"I don't think Vic ever meant anything by it. He had no children of his own and he just ..."

"It ain't my fault that he had no children of his own. If he'd stood up like a man, he could have had the woman he loved and all the family he wanted."

"I don't follow you."

"Don't worry about it. It's all old news anyway." H. V. gulped the punch and then said, "Somebody didn't send you over here to talk to me, did they?"

"No. Why would you think that?"

"Forget it. I'm just having an 'old man day.' Feeling sorry for myself. And then I see you walk in here, and I'm all better again. It's hard for me to think you're almost a preacher. Little Cal Vaxter, that boy next door who stayed in trouble all the time from morning till night. You don't get in trouble anymore, do you?"

"Oh, yeah. Just about all the time. You know, Mr. Stone, I often ..."

"Call me Hershel. And let me tell you, Little Cal, I'm proud of you for what you're making of your life. Religion ain't easy. And for it to be your life work ... well, I got all the respect in the world for you."

"Thanks. That means a lot. I always looked up to you when I was ..."

"You didn't look up to me for religion. I know that for sure. You know, Little Cal, there might be something about me you don't know even after all these years. Did you know I'm Jewish?"

"Well, Hershel, I know you have Jewish blood in your veins, but I don't know if you practice the faith."

There was a long but not really awkward break in the conversation. It was not as if one waited on the other as much as they both were waiting on a mutual meeting of the minds.

"You're right, son. Just the blood. I'm nothing. I haven't stepped a foot inside a synagogue since I was twelve years old. So I won't pretend. You know what bothers me most about all that? Esther. She was devout. Never missed a Sabbath. Then she hooked up with me, and I guess I pulled her down. Neither one of us have been in years and years. And Harlan ... I guess never. You ever talk to him about religion?"

"Yes. He's got a lot of questions."

"I never had many answers. Guess that's why I fell by the wayside. But then I don't put much stock in your side of the coin either. You guys, you Protestants. You annoy me."

"How so?"

"All of you read the same book, and then you get so many different meanings from it that you split up and have all kinds of brands of religion. Methodists. Presbyterians. Baptists. If there was one answer, there wouldn't be so many brands of Protestants."

They both found the humor and irony in this and again laughed together.

"You're right," Cal said. "We all read the same book and get different meanings from it. That's why it's so magical. It's all things to all people no matter what they're looking for. Your answer is in there and so is mine, even if we're asking different questions."

"But aren't we supposed to be looking for the same thing, son?"

"We never do. But the beauty of it is that we find the same thing."

"Not me. I guess there's not much hope for an old reprobate like me."

"It's never too late, Mr. ... It's never too late, Hershel. There's a parable about the laborers that ... "

"... *come to work early in the morning and then some later in the day and then some at the end of the day but they all receive the same reward.*" H. V. *finished Cal's sentence.*

Cal *smiled and in mock surprise said,* "*You've been reading the New Testament?*"

"*You'd be surprised at the things I know, son. But knowing it and believing it are two different things.*" H. V. *looked Cal intensely in the eye and asked softly,* "*Did you come over here tonight to save my soul?*"

"*No. I came over here tonight to see an old and dear friend. I came over here tonight to see the father of one of my best pals. To see the man who first gave me credit when I was fourteen years old so I could buy my girlfriend a bracelet for Christmas. Nobody can get credit at that age, and you knew that, even if I didn't. If I had never paid a cent, there was no way you could have collected. But you allowed me to establish a credit reference at twenty-five cents a week that has helped me and will help me all through my adult life. I came over here tonight to see the man who took me along on vacations to the beach more summers than I can count and gave me everything, penny for penny, he gave his own son and made me feel like an important part of the family. I came here tonight to see the man who picked my dog, King, up out of the street and carried him, cold and stiff, to the backyard so I wouldn't see him lying in the road when I came home from school. I'm not sure your soul is lost. I think you're just not real sure where it is.*"

H. V. *Stone reached over and held Little Cal Vaxter's hand so tightly his fingers turned white. Neither of them said a word, but the quietness of the room made the radio barely audible.*

The Senators had just pulled ahead with a home run.

CHAPTER FORTY-THREE

Vic and Arlo sat just outside the administrator's office door with the secretary, Fritz sitting between the two men, looking at neither but staring straight ahead at nothing in particular. Inside Arlo Stanley's office, Buddy sat behind the administrator's desk and dialed the hospital operator, asking to be connected to Harlan Stone's room. He waited as the phone rang twice. On the third ring, someone picked up.

"Hello."

"Darcy? This is Buddy."

"What have you found out?"

"I found Fritz."

"Where was he?"

"Here in the hospital all the time. I have him with me downstairs. How is Harlan?"

"Better. He's had something to eat this morning, and I think he's a little stronger."

"Good. Let me talk to him."

There was a pause and sounds of movement through the phone as Buddy waited for the receiver to change hands two floors above him.

"Hello."

"Well, if you're well enough to eat, you're well enough to get out of here."

"And when I do get out of here, the first thing I'm going to do is get something *decent* to eat."

"How about I bring you a cheeseburger from Mulligans for lunch?"

"Don't waste your time on a single cheeseburger. Bring me two."

"You got it. Now about Fritz. Darcy told you he was missing?"

"Yeah. That old fool. Where was he?"

"Sitting down here in the lobby. All day yesterday and last night. He's been here nearly as long as you've been here, I guess. I have no idea how he heard about what happened. I haven't gotten that out of him yet, but he refuses to leave and also refuses to come upstairs to see you. He just wants to 'sit vigilance' as he calls it."

"He is such an idiot. Dad was the only person in the world who could talk to him. He still won't say anything to me half the time. Just sits and looks at me. Of course, he still does good work. But what a dolt."

"Well, he's promised me if you talk to him on the phone, he'll let me take him home. So I'm going to put him on, and you say whatever you want—but then encourage him to go home. Okay?"

"Sure. Put him on."

Buddy walked to the outer office and motioned for Fritz. When he came in, Buddy handed him the phone and told him Harlan was on the line and wanted to speak with him. He stood close to Fritz and listened as they talked.

"This Fritz."

"Fritz? This is Harlan. I understand you've been concerned about me and I appreciate that. But I'm going to be all right. Everything is fine."

Harlan waited, apparently for a response, and when there was none, continued on.

"How did you hear so quick about what happened to me yesterday morning?"

"People talk at breakfast."

As Buddy listened, he had to think about that for a second to process what the old guy was meaning to say. That's how all conversation was with Fritz. He gave only what he wanted, and you had to figure out the rest.

"Oh. You mean you heard about it at breakfast. At Smitty's Diner where you eat every morning," Harlan asked.

"Smitty's. Yes."

"So anyway, Fritz, I'm going to be okay. Should be home in a few days and back to work pretty soon. You go on back home or to the store now. Buddy will take you wherever you need to go. All right?"

"You safe?"

"I'm safe. They're taking good care of me here. Darcy is with me, and I'm going to be just fine. Talk to you later. Good-bye."

There was no good-bye from the other end. Fritz simply handed the phone back to Buddy and walked out the office door, through the lobby, and out the glass front doors leading to the parking lot.

When Buddy and Vic came outside five minutes later, Fritz
was standing by the police cruiser, smoking a hand-rolled cigarette,
waiting for his ride.

CHAPTER FORTY-FOUR

The bride and groom, under the new identity of Mr. and Mrs. Harlan Stone, left directly from the country club for their honeymoon. She had wanted Niagara Falls, and he had argued vehemently for New York City. This war of words had gone on for months, and the only logical way to settle it seemed to be to favor both sides. They would drive to the Falls to spend two days and then continue on to the Big Apple for three nights of celebrating. This appeased if not pleased them both.

Their second day in upstate New York, Harlan sat on the balcony of their hotel and watched the tourists line up for the trek to one of nature's most fantastic water displays. He had been there just that morning with Darcy and didn't feel like going again that afternoon. Having water sprayed in his face was not something he cared to experience more than once. Darcy was lounging on the bed just inside the open sliding glass door in her light summer sweater and ankle-length skirt.

"Harlan, can you hear me?"

"I can hear you."

"Will you come in here?"

"What do you want?"

"I just want to ask you something."

"Go ahead. I can hear you."

"Harlan, are you happy?"

"I'm happy."

"I mean really happy. Are you glad we got married?"

"I'm glad."

"Really? Do you think you'll get bored with me?"

"No."

"Do you think I'm as pretty as I was when we first met?"

"Prettier."

"Harlan Stone, will you come in here where I can talk to you?"

He stepped inside and closed the sliding door behind him, shutting out all the outside sound. He walked to the bed, leaned over her, and kissed her.

"Is that all you've got to say?" she asked in her most sensual voice.

The days in New York City were just as much fun, if not more, for them both. They walked the streets, shopped, saw the sights, and even got in one full day of the World's Fair. They ate at Sardi's in the theater district and then farther uptown at the glamorous Stork Club. Harlan was able to get tickets to two of the year's biggest Broadway shows. They saw Katharine Hepburn, Joseph Cotton, and Van Heflin in The Philadelphia Story. *The next night they caught Ethel Merman and Betty Grable in Cole Porter's* DuBarry Was a Lady.

They were standing atop the Empire State Building at Fifth Avenue and West 34th Street, holding hands and marveling at the view.

"How long has this been here?" Darcy asked.

"This view or this building?"

"This building, silly."

"Not long. I think about eight years. It only took them a little over a year to build it."

"It sure is beautiful. You think when our marriage is a year old, you'll think I'm still beautiful?"

"I'm sure I will. Unless you just let yourself go and get to looking like an old washerwoman hag or something."

"It will never happen, Mr. Stone. I'll always keep myself beautiful for you and you alone."

They kissed, and she looked into his eyes, unaware or uncaring of the crowd around them. They were all strangers, and she'd never see them again in her life. She kissed him again and held him close to her as she did.

"You know what I wish?" she whispered in his ear.

"What's that?"

"That we were already on our way back to the hotel."

"Me, too."

"I mean it's a nice view and all. Don't get me wrong. But I'd rather look at you than all New York has to offer."

They were happy and in love, and the world was right with their hearts—their personal world, anyway. The real world around them was coming apart, and little did they know how that would soon affect their lives. But even more imminent was the crumbling that only the ring of a telephone can bring to a glorious happy occasion. They were in their room at the Park Tower Hotel on Central Park South when the call came.

"Hello."

"Harlan? This is Cal."

"Hey, pal. Don't you know you're not supposed to bother a man on his honeymoon?"

"I'm afraid I have some bad news. It's your dad."

"What's wrong?"

"He passed away at three thirty this afternoon."

There was a pause long enough for Darcy to realize what was happening. She didn't have to ask. She just went to her husband and put her arm around him while he continued to hold the phone.

"Are you still there?" Cal asked.

"I'm still here. Was he by himself?"

"Your mother and I were with him. She was there and called me. And when I went in the room he was already unconscious. I held one hand and she held the other, and he just sort of sighed real big and then passed. It was quiet and peaceful. We debated whether or not to call. I know you'll be starting home tomorrow, but your mother really wanted me to call you."

"Is she there?"

"She's downstairs with your aunt Vivian. But she's doing fine. She's a strong woman. I'll get her if you want to talk to her."

"No. Just tell her I'll call her in a little bit. And, Cal ... thanks, pal. I don't know what I'd do if you weren't there. Does Buddy know?"

"I'll call him next."

"We'll check out of here and leave for home right away."

Another chapter of Harlan Stone's life had closed with tragic results. He had inherited the family business at the age of seventeen because of his father's health and now he had become the head of the family at the age of twenty-three because of his father's death.

Back in Mt. Jefferson, Cal sat for a moment after hanging up the phone. There was more he wanted to tell Harlan, but he would wait until Harlan's mind was more receptive and his heart was more willing to understand.

CHAPTER FORTY-FIVE

While driving Fritz back to his room, Buddy tried to make conversation but was unable to encourage the old fellow to give anything more than grunts and two-word answers. Vic even chimed in and tried to help, but his questions produced only stares from the backseat. The grudge and resentment Fritz held for him had not waned with the years.

After dropping off Fritz and then Vic, Buddy went directly to his cubicle at the police station and looked up the number for Christopher, the older of the Drakos sons. He got him on the first ring.

"Christopher, this is Buddy Briggs with the police department. I'd like for you to come down to the station today. I need to talk to you."

"What's up, Briggs? Somebody park on a yellow line or something?"

"Yeah, something like that. What's a good time for you?"

"What if I said I'm busy and there is no good time?"

"I just want to talk to you, Christopher. Let's say one o'clock."

"Let's say two."

"Okay, two. Thank you very much, and have a good day."

Christopher Drakos hung up the phone without saying good-bye. But Buddy wasn't expecting good manners. He wasn't even sure he was expecting Drakos to show up at two o'clock.

But he did. Almost. At 2:20 he walked up to Buddy's cubicle and looked in.

"Knock, knock."

Buddy looked up from his desk and said, "Come on in and have a seat."

"Now what's so important I had to come all the way over here just to talk to you?" asked the dark man in the herringbone sport coat and pink tie as he sat down in the straight chair in front of the gun-metal gray desk.

"All the way over here?" Buddy grinned. "What is it, two blocks?"

"Whatever."

"Harlan Stone a friend of yours, Christopher?"

"No. He's a friend of yours."

"Do you have business dealings with him?"

"Have I ever bought jewelry from him? Yeah. I guess everybody in town has."

"He owe you money?"

"Now, what business is that of yours, Sergeant?" Christopher Drakos asked condescendingly.

"I can tell by your answer you didn't hear my question clearly. I'll ask you one more time. Does he owe you money?"

"People all over this town owe me money."

Christopher's left hand was resting on the edge of the government-issue desk, and he was tapping his fingers nervously to a rhythm apparently from somewhere inside his head. Lieutenant Briggs reached across the desktop and laid his hand on top of the tapping fingers to still them. When he spoke, he spoke softly and directly to the startled face in front of him: "Does Harlan Stone owe you money? And you'd better give me a yes or no answer this time."

Christopher stared at him long and hard before responding, but when he did he was succinct.

"No."

"Good. Does he owe anyone else in your family money?"

"You'd have to ask them."

"Do you owe him money?"

"Are you kidding?"

"You should know by now I'm not kidding."

"No."

"Where were you yesterday morning at five a.m.?"

"In bed with my wife. Where were you?"

"Drakos, I have copies of IOUs I found in Harlan Stone's safe. I think you have the originals. And I think if I search your house and your real estate office, I'll find them."

"You can make up anything and claim they're copies. That don't prove nothing, and you know it."

"We'll see. As of right now I'm putting you in custody and …"

"Wait a minute. You can't arrest me. You got nothing on me."

"I'm not arresting you. I can detain you in custody for twenty-four hours without arresting you. And while you're here, I'll get a warrant to search your house, your place of business, your brother's house and business, and your parents' house and restaurant. Then I'll call the newspaper and tell them what I'm doing because I'm sure they'd like to get pictures and maybe even get an interview with some of you about what's going on."

"You can't do that."

"Watch me. Tranium! Put this man in cuffs, and hold him till you hear from me."

"Just wait a minute," Christopher Drakos shouted as he jumped to his feet.

Buddy stood up at the same time and started around the desk just as Sergeant Tranium came barreling through the doorway.

"I said wait a minute," Christopher pleaded with his palms up in front of him. "I didn't come here looking for trouble today."

"Then where are the IOUs?" Buddy shot back at him.

"I never said there were any. If there is, I don't know about them."

"Does Harlan gamble with you? And don't give me one of your runaround answers."

"Sometimes, I reckon."

"Thursday night games or football lines or the track?"

"Some of all of those. But I don't know if he's in to us or not. Honest to God, I don't. I just don't know about all that."

"So that means your dad or your brother would have to know. Thank you, Christopher. You can go now."

"Wait a minute. I don't ..."

"You can go now. You just gave up your father and your brother to save your own hide. That's okay. I know they'll be happy to hear all about it. And believe me, I'll be happy to be the one to tell them."

Christopher Drakos stomped out of the cubicle and looked as if he would have slammed a door had there been one. Sergeant Tranium, who had been listening outside his cubicle, watched him till he cleared the building. Then Tranium turned to Buddy, who had already gone back to his swivel chair.

"You really got copies of IOUs on the Drakos family?"

"No."

"Umm. Nice move, Lieutenant. Nice move."

CHAPTER FORTY-SIX

Cal went back to Durham to seminary and his final year of studies. He carried a lot in his heart—and always a huge piece of Mt. Jefferson— wherever he went. Ellie had come home with him for Harlan and Darcy's wedding to meet his family. He took great pride in showing her around his hometown and introducing her to all his old friends. She and Amanda hit it off especially well, finding common ground as young working women in pre-war America. Ellie as a CPA and Amanda as a schoolteacher were the backbone of what would become a national structure in a few short years. Women—even those who were housewives just weeks and days before—became the norm in the workforce and professional positions. They were the young, female face of a changing nation that was about to see a transformation of responsibility and power. The "little woman," the "lady of the house," the "missus" would soon become the "head of the family," the "breadwinner," the "one and only parent" who not only would provide financially for the family but would be the emotional support and final word in all matters of the heart, soul, body, and spirit.

But these young men and women knew nothing of what was about to be expected of them. They were still in the throes of youth, enjoying the adventure and excitement of being on their own with the ones they loved by their sides. Cal and Ellie experienced these feelings daily while making plans to marry as soon as Cal finished seminary. And in the summer of 1940, they did both. The graduation was in Durham, North Carolina; the wedding was in Louisville, Kentucky. And all was sweet and well with the world.

They would only enjoy a year and a half of happiness before the world changed, but they had no way of knowing it.

"I know the wedding is only two weeks off, but I need to talk to you about something," Cal said one night over sandwiches at Ellie's apartment.

"The floor is yours, my love. Sweep me off of it."

"You may not be in this good of a mood after you hear what I'm about to say."

"Then hurry up. You're scaring me."

"I could put in for a church, and we could be settled into something within a couple of weeks after we get back from our honeymoon. But I've got something else in mind."

"After all that schooling, you don't want to be a minister?"

"Oh, yeah. Certainly I do. More than anything in the world. But there's a problem back home."

"Your mother?"

"Yeah. Ever since she and Dad bought my aunt and uncle out of the hardware store last year, they have had nothing but hard luck. With Mom taking sick these past few months, it's all on Dad, and to tell you the truth ... "

"... you want to go home and help your dad," Ellie said, putting a period on his sentence.

"Yeah. Instead of taking a church right now, I need to go back and give him some relief. I know that's not what we've talked about, but I really feel it's the right thing to do."

"Cal, if you take a church, we'd have to move anyway. I can do what I do any place we live. I don't care if I'm married to the village vicar or the local hardware man. So don't feel you have to sell me on it. I just don't want to live with your parents. Nor with mine, as far as that goes. Just promise me we'll have a place of our own, and we're there."

"Thank you, honey, for understanding. This takes quite a load off me. I've been carrying this for months."

"You should have said something. I'm going to be your wife. I'll always be with you wherever you go. So quit worrying about me. Understand?"

"I understand," Cal promised with a smile on his face.

She leaned across the table, kissed him, and said, "Mt. Jefferson, here we come."

And that was where the three Mulligans were when their idyllic world came to an end on December 7, 1941.

Harlan was managing Stones by Stone Jewelers on Main Street with help from Darcy, who was in and out of the store every day. His mother seldom darkened the aisles except for vacation times or when someone needed a day off. Maxine, who knew all the old customers and their extended families, was still his prime saleslady, and old Fritz still sat in the back room with the jeweler's glass in his eye and the green visor on his head. Harlan looked at himself every morning in the mirrored wall cases behind the counter and asked the image if he was becoming his father. He hadn't needed to ask. He knew he was. Same blue suit. Same white shirt and dark tie. Same green club ring on his right hand, third finger. Even the same stance at the back of the *store—one hand resting on the glass counter as he waited for the next customer to open the front door.*

Cal was just a couple doors up the street, deep into the Vaxter Brothers Hardware store; buying and selling products he had no interest in but happily helping out a father for whom he had all the love a son could have. His mother had become housebound and was seldom seen by anyone outside the family, while Ellie had taken a position with the Pennerwhite and Compton accounting firm, which had second-story offices above the drugstore just across the street. They ate lunch together nearly every day, usually at Mulligans, and rode home together every evening. It was only on weekends that Cal felt the loss of his chosen profession or divine calling. Most days he wasn't sure which it was; he only knew his life was on hold for a reason until he could pursue ministry with the honest ambition he felt in the depth of his stomach.

Buddy was busy helping Briggs and Son grow. They had employees to run the station and pump the gas and wipe the windshields and check the oil of all the cars that came through the driveway. They had at least one, sometimes two mechanics on duty every hour they were open—from 6:00 a.m. to 10:00 p.m. Sixteen hours, six days a week meant there were two shifts, and whenever anyone was out, it was up to Buddy to fill in even though he was busy keeping the books in the back office. Their new towing service was the only one in town and the surrounding county. This gave them so much business that they had to add another truck and driver to stand on call. Amanda was busy teaching her fifth-grade class at Hanna Cole Elementary, and their one day a week off together—Sundays—became sacred to them in more ways than one. Sometimes they would just disappear and not return to their little clapboard house with the blue shutters until after dark. But they were as happy each day as they were tired, and they were thankful for the prosperity and enjoyed the good times while they had them.

CHAPTER FORTY-SEVEN

It was three thirty in the afternoon; the dead time for all restaurants. The lunch crowd was gone, and the supper crowd was yet to be. A few coffee drinkers on a break from nearby businesses were scattered about, but most of the Mulligans staff were in the alley on a break of their own—smoking a cigarette and cooling off from a steamy kitchen. Vic was pouring iced tea in the back booth; first for Cal, then for Buddy. After he poured his own he sat down heavily and sighed at the pending subject.

"I went to see Harlan yesterday after we split up here. He was doing better," Vic said.

"I've talked to him since," Buddy interrupted. "We talked on the phone briefly this morning."

"Good. Because yesterday he was still pretty mad at you. Said you were treating him like a villain instead of a victim. Did you two patch it up this morning?"

"Can't say for sure. Our conversation was all about Fritz. I'll tell you about that later. But he seemed warm enough. Now, his wife's feeling toward me is a different story."

Cal smiled. "I'm sure." Then he continued with the wrap-up of his visit with Harlan. "The store's in trouble. He can't pay the bills. He stopped short of saying he was gambling in hopes of coming back financially, but if I had to guess, I'd say that's what's happening."

"I can add to that," Vic offered. "Nick practically threw me out of his restaurant when I came down on the Thursday night games. He was quick to tell me Harlan didn't owe him any money personally, but that was all he was willing to say. I had the feeling if there hadn't been customers at some of the tables, he would have gotten physical. Of course, just between us boys, I wish he had. As a matter of fact, I wish he had years ago."

Buddy and Cal looked at each other as Vic lifted his glass, drank from it, and set it down. Neither pursued what he meant by that last statement. Buddy was determined to keep the conversation on track.

"Funny Nick should say that. Christopher admitted Harlan didn't owe him any money either," Buddy said thoughtfully.

"They both could be lying," Cal said.

"Sure. But what if they weren't? That leaves only one other family member who might be out to collect a debt."

"Nicoli."

"He's the creepiest one of them all," Cal said.

"Yeah, and that's his best trait," Buddy said solemnly. "I think he's my next move. I'll call him in like I did Christopher and look him over."

"Be careful, son," Vic warned. "I never see him without a twenty-two caliber in his pocket."

"Odd you should say that, Uncle Vic. It was a twenty-two that took a piece out of Harlan's side."

No one answered Nicoli Drakos's phone. So Buddy went to his house in the Baymont section of town. It was the newest development and the most expensive. Houses were going up at an unprecedented rate and never-before-seen prices. Nicoli, a twenty-nine-year-old bachelor, had just built the biggest home yet in the curve of a cul-de-sac on a street he had bartered the city fathers to name after his family. 333 Drakos Drive. Buddy knocked on the front door. It swung open, and a man in his suit pants, suspenders, and undershirt stood with one hand on the door and the other on the door frame, defiant.

"What do you want?"

"I want to talk to you."

"Say it. But I don't have long. I'm busy."

"I'm not sure how long it will be. But I can tell you for sure, Drakos, it won't be over till I say it is."

"Come inside then. I have air conditioning in here, and I don't want it going out the door."

The house felt like a movie theater. Not too many houses in Mt. Jefferson had the luxury of cool air in the middle of June. The thought passed through Buddy's mind that this interview might take longer than he had originally thought it would. And he also felt this was not the place to hold it. Here stood Nicoli Drakos in the comfort of his own home, relishing the perfect temperature, causally dressed and at ease in familiar surroundings.

"Put your shirt on, Nicoli. We're going down to the station."

"What? You can ask me anything you want right here."

"I know I can, but I don't want to. Get a shirt."

"And if I don't?"

"I cuff you and drag you out of here by your feet. Now get a shirt."

Nicoli rode in the backseat of the police cruiser in total silence for the twelve-minute ride to the Mt. Jefferson police station. He walked in of his own accord and sat in the same cubicle and the same chair his brother had. Buddy took off his sport coat, loosened his black knit tie, and sat behind the desk.

"I've talked to my father and my brother. I know why I'm here. I have nothing to tell you they haven't already told you."

"They haven't told me anything. Except that Harlan Stone owed you gambling money."

"What? They told you that? No, they didn't tell you that. That's some sort of trick or something. Nobody told you that."

"What if I told you they even gave me a number?"

"I'd call you a liar to your face."

"Be careful, Drakos. Those are pretty strong words."

"My family wouldn't sell me out like that."

"Sell you out? Is that how you see it? They've sold you out. Given you up. You can't sell out an innocent man, Nicoli."

"No. That's not what I mean. Chris said you had a slick tongue. But you ain't tripping me up."

"Don't intend to, Nicoli. Just want some honest answers. Were you at Harlan Stone's house yesterday morning?"

"No."

"How did your fingerprints get on the back door and the kitchen sink?"

"I never touched the kitchen sink."

"You left traces all over that place. And I have a warrant here in my hand to search your house. And when I find a Halloween clown mask, you are sunk."

"You really got a search warrant?"

"Yeah. And you've really got a clown mask. So what do you say we get down to business? Harlan Stone is a good friend of mine, and I sorta want you to resist arrest. Do you hear me? I want you to put up a fight because there's nobody here but just us boys, and nobody will know but just you and me what really took place."

"Wait a minute, Briggs. I don't want to fight you. And you said I wasn't under arrest."

"Don't believe everything I say. Just look me in the eye and see if you think I mean what I say...."

"Lieutenant, here." A uniformed officer interrupted and walked to the desk and placed a sheet of paper on it. As he left, he winked at Buddy, who took his time reading the paper and then looked back at the perspiring man across from him.

"You know what this is?" Buddy asked.

"How would I know? You're the one reading it."

"It's the medical report stating it was a twenty-two–caliber pistol that shot Harlan. A Saturday-night special. That's what you carry, isn't it?"

"Who said I carry anything?"

"Come on, Drakos. We all know you've got something stuck in your belt every time you leave the house."

"Prove it."

"I've got the search warrant, remember."

"Yeah, but I don't have that gun anymore. So search all you want. You won't find nothing."

"Why did you get rid of it?"

"I didn't. I lost it somewhere. So if it shows up, I don't know where it's been. I'm reporting it stolen right now. Reporting it to you."

"That's a little late, don't you think?"

"Listen, Briggs. I didn't shoot nobody. I've never shot anybody in my life."

"But you carry a gun."

"Only carry. I've never had to use it."

"Until yesterday morning. Your car was seen parked in the Stones' neighborhood."

"That's all I got to say. Either I'm leaving here right now, or I want a lawyer."

"Things getting hot, are they, Nicoli?"

"I swear I'm leaving. Arrest me and let me call my lawyer, or I'm walking right now."

"Stone owe you money?"

"Yeah, he owes me money. Lot of people in town owe me. But I ain't ever shot any of them either."

"You can leave, Nicoli. We'll be watching you. And if you need a ride home …"

"I don't need nothing from you."

Nicoli Drakos stormed out through the police station, past the front desk and past a man leaning back against the wall in a straight chair, smoking the stub of a cigarette. The man pushed his straw dress hat to the back of his head and stood and watched as Nicoli rounded the corner of the building, heading apparently toward his father's restaurant.

CHAPTER FORTY-EIGHT

Mr. Vice President, Mr. Speaker, members of
the Senate and the House of Representatives;
Yesterday, December 7, 1941—a date which
will live in infamy—the United States of America
was suddenly and deliberately attacked by naval
and air forces of the Empire of Japan....

*Every radio in America was tuned to the presidential speech. Classrooms
and garages, department stores, factories and grocery stores, offices,
kitchens and living rooms. Every dial was turned to the president's voice,
and every person in America was listening with a grave expression. What
had been conjectured was now a reality. There would be tears and pain
and gnashing of teeth as mothers and lovers reluctantly let their loved
ones go, but the morning after the speech, there was only an eerie silence
and a sanctity that bonded strangers on the street. By noon, the front door
of city hall was a riot scene. Young and middle-aged men, eighteen to
forty, stood in line to sign up, proving they were American to the core. A*

few boasted and some even laughed to break the tension, but most stayed silent. But they all were of one mind and heart. A tumultuous blow had struck a safe and secure homeland, and its men were stepping up to take the responsibility of protecting all they cherished and held sacred.

Standing with the present and loyal were the three childhood friends. They were among those who held their silence and observed the attitude and mood of the men around them. Come their turn, they filled out the forms handed them and signed their names on the bottom line that would commission them into the United States Army "for the duration of hostilities" and would take them to places they could never imagine, physically or emotionally. Their families, though proud, were saddened by their commitment, and the next few weeks of freedom were spent in a dreamlike world of sharing and planning. Every moment of tenderness was exaggerated, and every hint of discomfort was diminished so as not to waste a moment of the cherished time they had together.

They were mailed a notice of induction for the date of January 4th, 1942. They still had one Christmas and one New Year's Eve at home, and both were spent quietly with wives and parents and other loved ones.

When Buddy walked into Mulligans at nine o'clock on the evening of January 2nd, Mabel Talley motioned him to the back booth, where the others were waiting. She locked the door behind him and began the process of closing up for the day. Harlan slid over, and Buddy sat down beside him and across the table from Cal and Vic.

"There's just nothing to say, boys," Vic said solemnly. "I'm lost for words. Except to say I'm proud of you. I'm mad at the reason you're leaving, but I'm proud of all three of you for doing what you're doing. I look at you sitting here, and I remember three little sneaking boys coming in here selling me my own bottles. I wouldn't have given you any odds

then that I'd be sitting here with you fifteen years later as men—men who have signed up to stand up and defend our country and maybe give your lives for it.

"That's what just breaks my heart tonight, fellows. If I could say, 'Well, we'll all meet back here in this booth when it's over,' it wouldn't be so bad. But I don't know that all or any of you will be back. This is no game. This is a war, and not everyone who leaves will come back. I'll pray every day you will, and I know your pretty little wives will pray too, and all your families. But our wills aren't always His will.

"I'll be here every day, so tell your women they can depend on Uncle Vic. I'll see none of them go without anything they need. And if I could go in your places, I'd do it in a heartbeat. I'm a fifty-year-old man. I've lived most of my life. It should be me instead of you. But that's not how it works.

"When you get on that train Sunday morning, you won't see me. I'll be there, but you won't see me. Those good-byes are for your families. So I'll tell you good-bye tonight. Plus I don't want you to see me as that train pulls out, 'cause I already know I won't be fit to be seen. I couldn't care for you boys more if you were all three mine. I suppose in a way you are. You're all I'll ever have. Don't know how long you'll be together after you leave here, but take care of one another if you can. As for me, I'll be in this booth every night by myself, waiting for you to come home. So see that you do. See that you do."

CHAPTER FORTY-NINE

No one came out of World War II unchanged. Some changed less than others, but all were forever carrying the burden of the times. You could see it in the faces of the women and the children. You could feel it on the streets of the big cities and the small towns like Mt. Jefferson. Everything was drab army green. Not just the posters and the products, but the attitudes and the mood. Teens grew up much too quickly. Women were overworked much too often. And the stress and heartache that filled each letter sent home and abroad was more evident with each passing day. Then the days became years.

Ellie was the first of the three wives to feel the change. When she knew that Cal was signing up, she felt sure he would enter as a chaplain. But the news that he didn't crushed her.

"Why wouldn't you?" she asked, her voice trembling. "Didn't you even ask about it?"

"Yes, I asked."

"Cal, you aren't considered a combat soldier if you go in as a chaplain. They can't fire on you. They can't hold you prisoner. All of that isn't just a myth, is it?"

"Not all of it. But ..."

"No buts about it, Cal. Chaplains are needed just as much as foot soldiers. Why in the world wouldn't you take the safest way; if not for yourself then for your parents and me?"

"Ellie, I can't go to war empty-handed. They gave me all the papers. But I handed them back. I can't march into combat with a group of men and be the only one without a gun. For heaven's sake, think about it. I don't want to tell my son one day that 'I fought the war, but, oh yeah, I didn't have a gun. The other guys took care of me.' I can't do that. You've got to understand."

"No, Cal. I have to accept it, but I don't have to understand."

Two months after he left on the train, Ellie moved back to Louisville to live with her parents. She told everyone it was to save money, but she was never sure if it was or not. She had become a part of Mt. Jefferson, but it had never really become a part of her.

Darcy's wartime job was a given. She would take over the jewelry store and run it as close to the way Harlan had as possible. The business had been through so many changes, she was sure it could weather another disaster. Harlan, their attorney, and their banking adviser had all assured her the store would continue to flourish if only she did nothing to hurt it. Management was not the problem. Overmanaging was the only harm she could do. She was well aware that there would be a dip in romantic sales. With so many husbands gone, there were few anniversaries and birthdays celebrated with the sparkle of jewelry, no matter the price or quality. Harlan had told her to concentrate on the youth. The preteens, the teens, the dating crowd. Show them interest, and appeal all the ads to them and to grandparents. Harlan knew his market, and Darcy learned it quickly. All this kept her occupied but was no partner for the loneliness she felt when she'd go home each night and close the door on the outside world. She, like millions of others, missed her mate and often cried herself to sleep.

Amanda's situation was more unique.

"Does anyone know?" she asked Buddy.

"Not from me. Have you told anyone?"

"I so want to tell my mother and dad before you ship out."

"We'll tell them together. But let's wait until the weekend before I leave. Let's get through Christmas and New Year's."

"Why wait?"

"Oh, I don't know, honey. Maybe I'm just scared to say it out loud too soon. Maybe I don't want to make myself too aware of it. I mean, this is something I always thought I'd be shouting from the hills. And now, here I am, trying to keep it quiet. I know it doesn't make sense."

"It's okay, Buddy. Nothing in the world right now is making sense."

"And to be honest, I'm scared to death. Not of where I'm going or what I have to do. But that we are about to bring a new life into this world at this time with the world in the shape it's in. What kind of life can we expect to give this baby? That's what scares me, and maybe I'm just not ready to face it yet."

"I understand, honey. I understand."

Their little girl was born five and a half months after Buddy left for induction. They named her Shirley Ann. She was three years old before he ever saw her and touched her face and felt her arms around him. He was happier then but still just as scared for her.

CHAPTER FIFTY

The man in the straw dress hat snubbed out his cigarette in a sand bucket by the front door. He walked back through the bustle of police headquarters to a small alcove where a man sat writing at his desk.

"You going to arrest him, Buddy?"

Without looking up, Buddy answered, "That's none of your business, Gary."

"Sure it is. When a guy like that is involved, it's everybody's business."

This time Buddy looked up. "Listen, Gary. We let you hang around here, pretty much with no strings attached. Mostly because if we didn't, you'd run a story about how the police department is trying to hide something. I know your game and in most cases respect it. But I told you early on, you've got to play by the rules. If somebody here says 'don't print it,' then you don't print it till it becomes a public story."

"Me printing it makes it a public story."

"Don't get cute, Gary. You know what I mean."

"And you've got to know what I mean, Buddy. That guy and his whole family—I mean, they're into everything, and nobody can seem to lay a hand on them. Now you've got something big on this guy, and I can't just let it go."

"You were out there listening to every word, weren't you?"

"Yeah. That's my job. I keep my eyes and my ears open. And then I warn the public. That's what a newspaper is all about."

"We're waiting on a couple reports to come back from Richmond, and then we'll know if this guy is who we're looking for. When that happens, I'll give you all I've got on it."

"From what you were saying to him, I thought you already had all those reports back from … wait a minute. Were you faking him out?"

"I'll give you something when we get it, Gary."

"You were, weren't you? Pretty slick, Lieutenant. You just out-Drakoed a Drakos. And it couldn't have happened to a nicer guy. That one, Nicoli, especially. He's scum. The old man … well, a lot of people like him. And Christopher, he comes and goes. But this one, he's scum. He went to school with my sister when they were kids. And he tried to force himself on her. She scratched him up pretty bad, but not bad enough. I was in France with you and a few other guys at the time. If I had been here, he'd have gotten more than scratches. He's scum. I can't let this one go."

"You're going to have to. If I had enough to arrest him at the moment, I would have him in the pokey right now. But I don't."

"When then?"

"Give me twenty-four hours."

"I don't know, Buddy. I want this guy, and I want him bad. It's hard not to nail him in the paper for everybody to see what he is."

"Be patient. Twenty-four hours."

"We'll see."

Gary Akerman pushed his straw dress hat back to the front of his head and fired up another Chesterfield as he cleared the front door and walked down the street.

Sergeant Tranium, who had heard the whole conversation, came to Buddy's door and said, "Mark my words. Akerman's going to be trouble."

"That's the problem with the law," Buddy said. "You can't stop somebody until they break it."

He sat at his desk with his hand on the phone. He knew if he called Judge Thompson and requested a search warrant for Nicoli Drakos's house and business, he would be refused for a lack of evidence. What he knew was only an assumption and, at best, a professional calculation. And Thompson wasn't famous for giving into either of those theories. Larger cities could afford that kind of investigation, but small-town judges tended to "protect and swerve." Another possibility would be to involve Chief Westover. He wielded more influence with Thompson, but getting the chief to act on a matter unfavorable to the Drakos family was next to impossible. Buddy had just come to the sad conclusion that waiting for morning was his only option when the phone rang under his hand and made him jump.

"Briggs."

"Buddy, this might be it. Shirley Ann is on her way to the hospital."

"How close are the pains?"

"Close enough she felt it was time to go. I'm leaving now. Are you going to be at the station or somewhere I can get in touch with you?"

"I'm leaving now too. See you there."

"Good-bye."

"Amanda?"

"Yes?"

"Is Louis Wayne with her?"

"He is. And thanks for saying his name instead of 'that boy' or 'her husband.' You might make it yet, Mr. Briggs."

"Don't give me too much credit. You should hear what I call him when you're not around."

"You're terrible. See you at the hospital. Love you."

"Love you, too. Bye."

CHAPTER FIFTY-ONE

All who knew them said Harlan came home the most changed. His rich, young good looks had given way to a cragginess that didn't kill his handsomeness but dampened the glamour. His hair lost its sheen, and his eyes were deeper and without the sparkle. He fell quietly back into the life he had left behind and never missed a day of turning the key each morning and night to the front door of Stone's. Very little change was made to the store in his absence, and very little was made on his return. The most noticeable was one made within a few days of his taking over his duties. He brought from home a portrait of his father that had been on the wall of his mother's den for years. He placed it on the back wall of the store, directly in sight of customers entering through the front door. There was H. V. again after all these years, at the back of the store, waiting on his customers. And there was his son, standing below him, waiting on whatever life dealt him next.

Cal was the only one of the trio to see action in the Pacific theater while the other two were in Europe. This was the longest separation any of them had experienced from their families and the longest from one another. But when Cal stepped on home soil again, he was ready with a renewed heart and spirit to finally begin the life for which he had so faithfully prepared. He and Ellie left Louisville for his first charge in Columbus, Ohio, with a feeling of personal drive and ambition neither had felt before. The three milestones he had imagined for himself were met in the first month of his tenure at the Hollybrook Methodist Church. Number one: He saw his name with the word Reverend in front of it on the marquee on the front lawn for the first time—a staggering and yet humbling sight. Number two: He joined his first couple in holy matrimony. He was more nervous than the groom, but he got through it without making a fool of himself. (The fact that the marriage ended in divorce eighteen months later was a joke his congregation never let him forget.) And number three: He officiated his first funeral. It was for an old man who hadn't darkened the door of the church for years even though he was still a member. He had no family and few friends. There were eleven people in the pews and one new minister in the pulpit who had to do a lot of inventive speaking to fill the allotted time.

His mother had passed while he was in service, but their visits back to Mt. Jefferson remained frequent, as his father still lived there and was still able to oversee the management of the hardware store. For Cal, unlike for Ellie, the little town was still very much a part of him.

Briggs and Son had sailed right along during the four years Buddy was gone. Chub had hired help to take over Buddy's duties, and those things were being done well. And Buddy was glad because he knew he wanted to do something else with his life. He had learned to fly in the service and once considered reenlisting and making a career of it. But he decided against that route, and he fell comfortably back into the life, *if not the occupation, he had left behind. A friend from school had first mentioned the MJPD to him two days after he came home. Amanda appeared shocked at his consideration of this suggestion but offered little resistance when he decided to pursue it. That first day in the new blue uniform almost made him change his mind. He had sworn many a day to himself, while in service, that he would never wear a uniform again. He disliked the restrictions the police uniform offered but always respected the essence of its demands. He only wore it for two years. When a new detective division was established, he was appointed head of it and became one of only two plainclothesmen on the force.*

Getting acquainted with his three-year-old daughter was the joy of his life. The rumpled pictures he had carried all over Europe did no justice to her sweetness and beauty. She was a miniature of her mother, and he loved them both with an equal and undying passion. He lived for his girls, and life, thank God, was good again.

CHAPTER FIFTY-TWO

Amanda was in the waiting room. There were other people around her, but none Buddy recognized as being a part of their circle of family or friends. The same kinds of people always seem to be in an emergency-room waiting area. The young mother with two rowdy kids who hang all over the chairs and roll on the floor until the exasperated mother yells at them and attracts twice the attention their antics have attracted. The elderly couple quietly reading the magazines offered and occasionally whispering secrets of comfort to each other. The restless, anxious, and worried family member who keeps going to the nurses' station to ask inane, implausible questions, searching for a modicum of comfort.

And always the one who is pacing and smoking and getting a drink from the water fountain and walking to the window and then back to his seat, just to start the same cycle again moments later.

"Have you been back?" Buddy asked as he sat down beside Amanda.

"Not yet. Louis Wayne and one of the nurses took her back. I'm just waiting till I catch someone's attention at the desk, and I'll ask them what the status is. They don't seem too busy. How about you? You doing okay?"

"I'm fine."

"You talk to Harlan today?"

"On the phone. I thought I'd go up and see him after we get through down here."

"What about the twins, honey? Don't you think we should be with Darcy when they get home from camp? Be with her when she tells them?"

"Sure. But there's time for that. They're not due back for a few days."

"Have you eaten supper?" Amanda asked, knowing he hadn't even thought about it.

"No. You want to get something in the cafeteria here?"

"Sure. As soon as we hear some— Here comes a nurse now."

The RN approaching them was short with coal black hair. Her skin looked like pasteurized milk. Her eyes were so dark they glistened as the fluorescent lights hit them. Her mouth smiled easily and with a warmth that lit up her face. She was a walking beauty with a personality to match.

"Mr. and Mrs. Briggs?"

"Yes," Amanda said.

"I thought I recognized you. I'm sure you two must be excited."

"Oh, we are. Is everything all right back there?"

"That's what I came out to tell you. Everything is fine. As a matter of fact, I don't look for much of anything to happen soon.

The doctor has seen her. She's having pains, but they are not as often as they were when she first came in. So he thinks we might be in for a little bit of a wait."

"That's fine," Amanda assured her. "We'll wait."

"But that's what I wanted to tell you. If you need to go anywhere, just leave me your number, and I'll be glad to give you a call should something begin to happen."

"We were thinking about going down to the cafeteria and eating supper."

"Certainly. Why don't you do that. I'll come get you if something happens. But just between you and me, I don't think it will. You'll have plenty of time to eat. Just ask for me at the desk when you come back, and I'll come out and catch you up. My name is Korina."

"Thank you, Korina. I'm Amanda, and this is my husband, Buddy."

"Yes, I thought so. Nice to see you. You both go have a nice dinner. I'm on duty till midnight, and I've been assigned to your daughter, so don't worry about a thing. She's in good hands. And Dr. Sanderson is back there, and he's the best."

"Thank you so much. We'll see you in a little bit."

As they walked off toward the elevator to go to the hospital cafeteria, which was open for both the employees and the public, Amanda spoke in low tones to her husband. "I thought I recognized that girl."

"Really? Who is she?"

"You don't know?"

"She looks familiar, but, no, I can't say I know her."

"When she told me her first name, then I knew for sure who it was. Korina Drakos. She's the youngest. The only girl if I'm not mistaken. Isn't that right?"

Buddy didn't answer right away. His mind was too full to allow his mouth to operate at the moment.

CHAPTER FIFTY-THREE

The crowds downtown were bigger than ever. Storefronts that had been empty while Buddy was growing up were full—not a vacant one in sight. Mt. Jefferson reflected the boom all of America was experiencing two years after the war. It was rare to find a good parking space anywhere on Main Street, and that was both good and bad for the local businesses. However, parking was the least of Buddy's worries this particular day because where he was headed was within two blocks of the police station, and he enjoyed the walk.

Every window he passed sported an American flag. It was just two days till the Fourth of July, and all of the merchants had come out for it in a big way. Banners and bunting adorned every building; red, white and blue blazed up and down each street. It had been this way both Independence Days since they had come home. It saddened him, the memories a furling flag brought to his mind, but it made him happy to know the citizens appreciated the costly freedom they still enjoyed. He smiled and spoke to nearly everyone in his path until he reached his destination. He pushed on the glass door, held it for a woman and a little girl coming out, and then looked up and saw the familiar figure of the proprietor standing at the counter at the rear of the store.

"Did you come in here to buy something or to shoplift?" the man in the back yelled the length of the store.

"That depends on how I'm treated," Buddy shot back while walking toward him.

"I'll treat you the same way I treat everybody. I'll get all I can before you get out of here." Harlan laughed as a couple of customers turned and smiled at the banter.

"No, to tell you the truth, I really am here for a special reason. My anniversary."

"No kidding. Which one is it?"

"The tenth."

"Oooh. That is a special one."

"What is the tenth one supposed to be? You know, paper and wood and all that stuff."

"Diamonds!"

"Really? Diamonds?"

"I'm asked that question about six times a week, and the answer is always diamonds. 'What's the third anniversary?' Diamonds! 'What's the fifteenth anniversary?' Diamonds! Doesn't matter which anniversary it is, I'm going to sell them something with a diamond in it."

"Okay, so what do you have? And show me the price first."

"You don't have to worry about the price. You pay whatever I pay. Just look around and see what you like. Necklaces and bracelets over here. Earrings and watches over here. Or maybe a bigger diamond to set into her original engagement ring. You tell me, and we'll fix you up."

While Harlan was talking and Buddy was bent over looking through the glass tops at all the glitter within, Buddy heard the bell that dinged every time someone opened the front door. He looked up just to see who came in, not so much out of curiosity as out of a cop's instinct to know what's going on behind him. He saw a man dressed in a gray pinstriped suit, carrying a newspaper under his arm. Nick Drakos. Buddy went back to his shopping, and Nick stayed at the front of the store as if waiting for someone or something. Harlan continued to talk, instructing Buddy on the items he was looking over and directing him to others he might like. After a while, he heard Nick say in a voice loud enough to carry to the back of the store, "I'll come back after while," and then he left with a ding again.

"What's that all about?" Buddy asked with complete innocence.

"Just Nick being Nick. He probably had a list of the specials he's running this week. He drops them off sometimes so we'll know what's cooking each day."

"Why didn't he drop them, then? He leave because I was in here?"

"Why would you think that? I guess he just wanted to say something but saw I was busy."

"Just seems a little strange."

"Hey, don't put me in the position of defending Nick Drakos. He's a man all to himself. Just ask Uncle Vic if you don't think so. I eat lunch at Nick's place sometimes, but I'll be the first to tell you he and his boys are some odd characters."

Buddy let it go and went back to the matter that brought him in to begin with.

"So what really is the tenth anniversary?" he asked Harlan.

"Tin, I think. But who wants to buy their wife something tin? I mean, a drinking cup? A picture frame? Or some cheap candle holders?"

"*Maybe I could find something at the hardware store. Or I could consider that bracelet right there.*"

"*That's a good choice, my man. You want it gift wrapped?*"

"*Sure.*"

"*When is it? I should know. I was there, but ...*"

"*Next week. The eighth.*"

Harlan turned serious. "*Ten years. And here it is 1947. Hard to believe, isn't it? Think where we were just five years ago. Do you think about it much?*"

"*No.*"

"*Don't know how you do it. You live in the moment, don't you? Wish I could.*"

Buddy left the bracelet to be wrapped and promised to pick it up later that afternoon. As he walked by the Drakos restaurant, he glanced in the window and saw Nick at his usual table, smoking and reading the paper. He wasn't sure why the man's visit to Stone's bothered him so much. But it did.

CHAPTER FIFTY-FOUR

Buddy was in the hospital as a patient only once. He'd had an appendectomy a few years before and had to spend two nights and three days in one of the sterile rooms for two on the third floor. Nothing about the stay was pleasant—certainly not his roommate, a local barber who was having a gallbladder operation and who tended to snore all night. Nothing and no one could stop the snoring until the morning sun crashed through the window and woke the man. But this was the least of his annoying habits. The one that bothered Buddy most was the way he read the morning paper and his Luke Short western novels. He read them aloud. And loudly. People in the rooms on both sides of them could hear him. Buddy had tried to play the radio to drown him out, but it only served as competition, and the radio finally lost. But even among all these bad memories, what he remembered most clearly from his ordeal was the hospital food. And this is what led him to say to Amanda over dinner in the hospital cafeteria, "How can the food be so good in here and so bad upstairs?"

"I'm sure it all comes from the same kitchen."

"You don't really believe that do you?"

"Certainly. It's just that upstairs, you're not feeling well, and it makes dinnertime seem more like medicine than a meal."

"That's a good theory and one I'll consider. I don't intend to agree with it, but I'll consider it."

They both laughed.

"Are you going to try to see Harlan while we're here?" Amanda asked.

"Sure. You want to go up with me?"

"I'd love to. Maybe Darcy will be there. I haven't talked to her today."

"Let me warn you before we go—Darcy may not be too happy with me."

"What happened? What did you do to her?" Amanda asked almost scoldingly.

"I accused her of not telling me the whole truth."

"You didn't. Why would you do that?"

"Because some things are not adding up. I don't think whoever it was came to rob them. I think he came to threaten Harlan."

"And what makes you think she knows more than she's telling?" Amanda asked with more understanding.

"Because she was there and saw it all."

"And you said this to her face?"

"I'm a cop, honey. That's what I do. It doesn't accomplish anything if I don't say it to their face. And since I've told you this much, you might as well know she pretty much threw me out of the house."

"What?" Amanda couldn't believe what she was hearing.

"She picked up my coffee cup, told me I was through there, and turned and went upstairs. Left me sitting in the kitchen with the dog."

"So if she's up there in Harlan's room, you don't want to see her?"

"That's not it. I don't care either way," Buddy assured here. "I just wanted you to know what was going on in case there was any kind of scene. Believe me, I'm prepared to stand behind what I had to say to her. And it might not be over. I may have to talk to her that way again."

"Oh, Buddy, I hope not. She's so ..."

Their son-in-law interrupted them as he walked through the door to the cafeteria and over to their table.

"Hey, folks."

"Hi, Louis Wayne," Amanda said. "Do you have news?"

"Yes and no. They sent me down here to find you and tell you we're going home."

"Home? What's happened?"

"Nothing. That's just it. The doctor said it's a false alarm. The labor pains are practically gone. He says it happens all the time. Could be days yet. So they're letting her go home."

"We're about through. We'll come with you," Amanda said.

"That's okay. You go ahead and finish eating. I'll take care of Shirley Ann. Then you can go up and see your friend. How is Mr. Stone?"

"He'll live," Buddy answered.

They said their good-byes, and Amanda and Buddy sat at the table and watched him go. He had just cleared the doorway when Korina Drakos walked through another entrance.

"Did you get the message about your daughter?" she asked.

"Yes," Amanda said. "They're sending her home."

Buddy noticed again her hypnotic eyes and beautiful skin. She stood with her hands on her hips while talking to them and flashed a smile and a hello at everyone who passed. He didn't hear all she was saying, but when he tuned back into the conversation between her and Amanda, he noticed Korina was looking directly at him.

"Excuse me, what did you say?" Buddy asked.

"I said 'You have the evening free, and you can take your wife to a movie tonight.'" Korina said with a smile.

"Yeah, that sounds like fun." Buddy chuckled. "But we've got visiting to do while we're here."

"That's right. Your friend is here, isn't he? I hope he pulls through that all right."

"Thank you. And thank you for your help with our daughter."

As she walked away and they were getting up from the table, Amanda spoke. "She is so pretty, isn't she?"

"Yes, she is. But that's the second thing I see when I look at her. The first thing is—she's a Drakos."

"And that's always bad?"

"Well, it ain't always good."

CHAPTER FIFTY-FIVE

Their first year in Columbus, a daughter, Elizabeth, was born to Cal and Ellie. Two years later, they had a son, Matthew, and Cal was sure this was only the beginning of the large, houseful of children he had wanted since he was a child. With no brothers and sisters, he had spent a lot of lonely nights and weekends growing up. No one had noticed because of his inseparable friendship with Harlan and Buddy. But having a brother or sister to lean on and share with was a dream he'd never told anyone. Certainly not his parents. They had showered him with everything they could afford as far as money, time, and love were concerned, but he always wondered what it would be like to have a sibling who knew the family secrets and shared the closeness and warmth of a small home. He hoped he could give that secure and belonging feeling to his children, no matter how many there might be.

After four years, the denomination encouraged a move, and Cal and his family ended up in a farming community in rural Pennsylvania. The church was just outside Lancaster, and the powers that be in the Methodist denomination allowed them to stay there for five years. The kids loved the place and made lots of friends. Ellie even warmed up to a few women's circles and put more of herself into the effort than she had in Columbus. But then in 1954 it was time to move again.

"Cal, this is ridiculous."

"I know how you feel, Ellie, but ..."

"But do you care how I feel? Do you care how the children feel?"

"Of course I do. But this is the life in the Methodist church. We move."

"Why? Why do you have to move every four or five years? Don't they know we have a family?"

"Yes, they do. And you knew this was the custom of the denomination before we ever had a family. Before you ever married me."

"Maybe I just didn't give it proper thought. But I'm giving it proper thought now."

"What are you talking about? Giving what proper thought? The church or marrying me?"

There was a long pause; she seemed not so much to gather the words but to try to make sure he understood the weight of them. "All of it. The kids come first, and if you would take time to talk to them and consider them, you'd know how they feel about it."

"I have talked to them. And I've tried to explain the situation. Not like you do when you just support whatever view they have at the time. I've tried to show them the responsibility I have and that I can't just up and change something because it doesn't suit our family."

"Cal, they are six and eight years old. Matthew has just started to school. Elizabeth has close girlfriends, and you can't just uproot them and take them all over the country like this for the rest of their lives."

"If I were military, we'd have to do this. If I were in a national company with offices all over the world, we'd have to do this. There are lots of families in our situation. We are not unique."

"Oh, yes, we are. We're nomads. Gypsies. Wandering all over the place. Never owning a home. Living in one rented parsonage after another. Wouldn't I just love to have a house of my own to fix up the way I want it for a change."

"I have nothing more to say unless you want me to quit and get a job teaching. Or driving a bus or whatever you might have in mind for me. I never kept this from you. You knew from day one who I was and what I was. You knew the policy, and you came into it with eyes wide open."

"Yes, I did. But I didn't know then I would feel this way. I didn't know then we'd have kids who wouldn't feel the same way you do about just picking up and moving on a moment's notice. No, Cal, I need something more. Something more than this. I want a home of my own."

"Maybe the next place we'll be able to stay longer."

"Why couldn't you have been a Baptist or a Presbyterian? Some of those men stay for twenty-five and thirty years at the same church. Their kids grow up and have the same friends all the way through school."

"I can't change the things I can't change, Ellie. It's that simple."

They didn't talk about it again for three weeks. The next time the subject came up, Cal used the only weapon he had. He was tied to the customs and laws of the church, and yet he wanted to make and keep his family happy. And that, peeled down to the core, meant he had to find a way to make Ellie happy.

As he sat on his side of the bed, taking off his shoes after Elizabeth and Matthew had gone to sleep, he watched his wife do her nightly routine at her vanity table.

"I had a meeting today and made some phone calls concerning our next move." He waited for a reaction from her, but when none came, he continued. *"There are a number of good places open. Upstate New York near Buffalo. A couple back in Ohio, but I knew you wouldn't want that. There're two or three in the Carolinas. But then there was something else that looked really good."*

This time he waited her out. He was silent until she finally turned around and looked at him and asked, *"Where?"*

"Ashland, Kentucky. Just two hundred miles from your mom and dad. They could be with their grandchildren weekends, Christmas, all summer if they wanted. What do you think?"

"Sounds fine," she said with no emotion or excitement in her voice—but no anger either. *"When would we go?"*

"January."

"I'll tell the kids tomorrow."

"Let's tell them together."

"That's okay," she said, combing her hair and staring into the mirror. *"I'll tell them."*

CHAPTER FIFTY-SIX

Amanda was in the kitchen fixing breakfast. Buddy walked through from the bedroom and out the back door to get the newspaper from the driveway. Each morning when he found the daily paper folded into a perfect square with each edge tucked into its own invented flap, he smiled. This was the same fold he had given newspapers on his paper route so many years ago. You could make them sail, and the heavier the news, the more accurate the toss. Their paperboy was pretty good. The paper was in the same place every morning except for only a couple of times when it had hit the car and bounced into the shrubs.

Buddy didn't open the paper until he sat down at the table with his coffee in front of him. He skimmed the headlines and the pictures on the front page; Queen Elizabeth was on a forty-five–day tour of Canada; a federal court had ruled that Orval Faubus, governor of Arkansas, had illegally closed the public schools there; Branch Rickey was announcing plans for a third major baseball league and was going to call it the Continental League—see Sports Page for more.

But it was the small story in the lower right-hand corner that caught his eye. The bold headline simply said:

Local Realtor Questioned In Shooting

Local realtor Nicoli Drakos, of Drakos Brothers Realty, was questioned yesterday in the shooting of Mt. Jefferson merchant Harlan Stone. Stone, owner and operator of Stones by Stone Jewelry, was shot in his home at 2244 Eagleton Lane Wednesday morning in the early a.m. by an intruder. He is recovering in the hospital, and his condition is listed as stable.

Drakos, 29, a lifelong resident of the area, was questioned and released by the MJPD. He was not available for comment. The *Daily Press* considers this an ongoing investigation and will report accordingly as the story develops.

Buddy never even looked at page two. He got up and went straight to the phone and dialed the station. The desk sergeant answered on the first ring.

"Mt. Jefferson Police."

"Who is this?"

"Tolley. How can I help you?"

"Jim, this is Briggs. I need you to make a call. Call Gary Akerman, and tell him I want to see him."

"The newspaper guy?"

"Yeah. Try him at his office or at home. But find him and tell him I want to see him at the station in thirty minutes flat. Got it?"

"Yes sir. Consider it done."

But it wasn't done. While Buddy had finished dressing and was considering skipping breakfast altogether, the phone rang. It was Sergeant Tolley again.

"Lieutenant, I found him. But there's a problem."

"What's the problem?"

"He won't come."

"What do you mean he won't come? He told you that?"

"Yes sir. He said he's afraid to come. He said he knows why you want him, and he isn't coming in here. He said if you wanted to see him he'd meet you somewhere in public, but he will not come in here and see you in private. I think he's real scared."

"He's got reason to be."

"You want me to go get him?"

"No. Tell him I'll meet him in public. I'll meet him at Mulligans in the back booth at eight thirty sharp. And Tolley, stress to him how I feel about punctuality."

"I get your meaning, Lieutenant. I'll take care of it. He'll be there, or he won't be anywhere."

"Thank you, Jim."

Buddy stood for a moment and looked through his window at the beautiful flowers in his backyard. He hated to get mad this early in the morning. And such a pretty morning too.

At 8:29 a.m. Gary Akerman walked cautiously through the front entrance of Mulligans. He was met by Vic Princeton, who called him by name, greeted him, and directed him to the back booth on the right. There he found Buddy Briggs. There was no coffee on the table, no donuts, nothing that would suggest social amenities of any kind. This was strictly a business meeting.

"Sit down," Buddy said with no expression.

"Buddy, I know you're mad, but let me explain."

"There's nothing to explain. I told you not to do something, and you did it."

"I can explain. Just give me a chance. I went back to the office, and I admit—I wanted to write the story. I wanted to real bad 'cause I don't like Drakos. I went back to the office, and I mentioned it to Riley, the editor, and he thought it would be a good story. I told him what you had said, and he gave me this long lecture about what makes a good newspaperman and how you can't ever let anybody stifle the story. That's what he kept saying. 'You can't stifle the story.' By this time I really didn't want to do it, but I had already mentioned it to him and he wouldn't let it rest. I mean, come on, Buddy, he's my boss. I couldn't just not do it."

"You could have just kept your mouth shut to start with."

"I wish I had. But it was too late then. I had to go with it or risk getting on the outs with my boss."

"You tell a real sad tale, Gary. And I'm not buying any of it. And even if I did, it wouldn't matter because I don't care about Riley or anybody else you've got to deal with. And right now you shouldn't care about anybody else but me. Because you know what I'm going to do? I'm going to ban you from the police station. No more sitting around waiting on police calls and getting in on the ground floor on fights and wrecks or whatever scandal gets you all hot and worked up. No more favoritism. You will not be able to step foot inside that place until you get written permission from me."

"Don't do this, Buddy. Don't do this to me."

"You have disrespected my wishes and disrespected me. And you have put a citizen in harm's way and his reputation in jeopardy."

"Aw, come on, Buddy. We're talking about Nicoli Drakos here. What do you mean his reputation is in jeopardy? You couldn't damage his reputation if you poured acid on it."

"You miss the point, Gary. The point is I asked you to do something as a friend and an associate, and you thumbed your nose at me."

"My boss made me do it."

"Your mouth made you do it. If you had kept it shut you wouldn't be in this situation now."

Vic stepped up to the table and quietly said, "Buddy, there's an officer here to see you. Tolley. Says it's urgent."

Jim Tolley rushed toward the booth and, with a red face from running, blurted out, "Buddy, we got a problem. A call just came through. Somebody else just got shot."

"What? What happened?"

"Nicoli Drakos."

"Who did he shoot?" Buddy asked as he slid out of the booth.

"No. He's the one that got shot. In his office."

"When?"

"Just now. Just minutes ago."

Buddy started for the door and then stepped back and looked at Gary Akerman still sitting in the booth, his head in his hands.

"Where were you just before you walked in here?" Buddy asked in official tones.

"You don't think I did it, do you?" Gary said with a tear in his voice.

"Oh, you did it, all right. I just don't know yet if you pulled the trigger."

"Lieutenant," Sergeant Jim Tolley said in a whisper, "it wasn't him. They've already got the shooter."

CHAPTER FIFTY-SEVEN

The first Monday night of January 1959, the administrative board of the Mason Street Methodist Church met at the usual time, 7:30 p.m., and in the usual place, the Prophets Sunday school room in the church basement. This was the largest of all the classrooms, it was closest to the minister's study, and it was the only room that had padded seats on all the chairs. The Reverend Paul Franklin presided and, after having the minutes from the previous meeting read, asked for any old and new business. When each item had been presented, discussed, and closed, he stood nervously among the group of twelve men and in a quiet and dry voice asked for their attention.

"Gentlemen, before we adjourn this evening's monthly meeting, I have something I need to say to you. Due to personal and professional circumstances, it is my very unpleasant duty to announce to you tonight that my family and I are officially in search of a new charge. Just this morning I have put in with the bishop for a new church and location. It's one of the hardest things I have ever had to do because, as I hope you all know, I have come to love this congregation and this town. Everyone here has become my friend, and every family here has become a part of

my very self. It brings me great anguish to stand here before you and say these words tonight, but I feel I must. So this is my official notice. My wife, Dove, my daughter, Millie, and I all feel a great sadness in leaving, but we want you to know that we hold each of you and every member of this church in the highest esteem. You will be forever in our hearts wherever we may go."

There were many questions asked and many statements made that reassured the Reverend Franklin he would be missed. Paul Franklin graciously left the meeting before they adjourned so the board would have a moment to discuss the future of the church without his presence.

"What's our next move?" one of the younger members asked.

"We notify the bishop that we are looking, and then we're sent names and résumés to view, and the whole process begins," said one of the older fellows.

"How long will it take?" someone else asked.

"Hard to say. Months, for sure."

"Where do we find an interim minister?" another asked.

"They'll provide one, or we can get others locally to fill in till we get the right man."

Buddy Briggs listened to the discussion with great interest, but he was already thinking of a possible solution. When the right time came, he spoke. "Gentlemen, I have an idea. Do most of you remember a man who was born and raised here in Mt. Jefferson, Cal Vaxter?"

Most said they did. A couple of the newer fellows were not familiar with him but had heard the name.

"Well, he's a native, he's a Methodist minister, and he was raised in this church. Right now he's in Ashland, Kentucky. But I've often thought how nice it would be if he were back here in an official capacity. If all of you

think it's a good idea, I'd like to contact him and see if we could forego a lot of the procedure. If he's interested, we could take his name to the bishop and maybe get this thing done with a minimum of red tape and waiting."

The discussion was sparse and the vote was unanimous, and Buddy was handed the duty of handling the entire situation on behalf of the council.

"Hello."

"Cal, this is Buddy."

"Buddy! Hearing your voice is exactly what I needed today."

"Why? You having a rough one?"

"Oh, yeah. But you didn't call to hear my problems. To what do I owe the honor?"

"Paul Franklin announced to us last night that he's leaving."

"I'm sorry. Paul's one of the good guys. Where's he going?"

"Don't know that yet. He doesn't even know yet. He's had a lot of family problems lately. To tell you the truth, I wasn't all that surprised. I think he wants a fresh start for his wife and his daughter. But all that aside, the reason I'm calling is this: Would you be interested?"

The pause was longer than Buddy had expected. Long enough that he changed his mind at least three times on whether he was going to hear an exuberant yes or a flat no. When it came, it was neither.

"Do you think that's a good idea, Buddy? I mean, am I the right man for this?"

"Who better?"

"You know what I mean. So many of those folks knew me as a kid. As a teen. And they might not feel as comfortable with me in that

position as they would a total stranger. Sometimes there's a benefit in hiring a stranger. The congregation doesn't know his faults, and he doesn't know theirs. They both kind of start off with a clean slate."

"I think you're overanalyzing it. But the first question is, would you feel uncomfortable?"

"I'd have to think about it. But my first question is, what would they feel?"

"Okay, I'll make you a deal. First, let me assure you the board is all for it. But here's how it'll go. You think about it, and let me handle the congregation. I'll take it to them, get an honest reading, and let you know."

"Even if it's negative?"

"Even if it's negative. But it won't be. And I'll call you next Monday after I've polled the congregation."

"Sounds like you're moving pretty fast on this thing. But, yeah, that's fair. I'll definitely think about it and pray about it. Let's talk Monday. How are Amanda and Shirley Ann?"

"Just great. And Ellie and Elizabeth and Matt?"

"Kids are fine. I won't know how to answer about Ellie till after I break this latest news to her."

They both laughed but not joyously. Buddy could tell there was more truth than humor in what he said.

"Do you see Harlan?" Cal asked.

"All the time."

"Tell him I'll call him sometime next week. Elizabeth has a birthday next month. She finally becomes a teenager. And I want to get her something appropriate. You've got a teenage daughter. What's a good gift?"

"Anything shiny. That goes for a female any age."

They laughed some more and talked briefly of other family and friends and hung up with the promise of resuming their conversation the next Monday.

Chapter Fifty-Eight

Buddy arrived at Drakos Brothers Realty less than six minutes after leaving Mulligans. Two police cars, a paddy wagon, and an ambulance were blocking the street at the front door. Flashing lights attracted attention from everyone who crept by. He parked with two wheels on the sidewalk and jumped out of the car, leaving it unlocked and vulnerable to traffic. The first person he saw was Officer Tranium.

"Two shootings in three days, Lieutenant; we're starting to look like a big city," the officer said.

"Tell me about it. What happened?"

"Two to the chest—close range."

"Is he dead?"

"No. They're bringing him out right now. He's going to live. He's too mean to die."

"What kind of gun?"

"Twenty-two caliber. We have it."

"I understand you have the shooter, too. Where is he?"

"Secured in one of the offices inside. You want to see him?"

"Sure. Let's go."

They walked inside and past the other policemen already on the scene. A secretary was sitting at her desk, blotting her eyes with a tissue. She looked as if she was about to be sick.

"Somebody better take care of her," Buddy said to Tranium. "Just point me to the right door, and you see after the lady at the desk."

Tranium pointed to the closed door that said Private, and Buddy walked ahead and turned the knob. He entered what appeared to be a small conference room with an eight-foot table and six soft chairs around it. Standing by one of the curtained windows was a uniformed cop, and sitting in one of the chairs was the man he had come to see.

"What's going on here?" Buddy demanded.

Fritz looked up with a blank expression on his face and then back down at the floor.

"Fritz. What's going on?" Buddy repeated.

"He hasn't said a word since we got here," the uniform offered.

"Fritz. You've got to talk to me. What did you do?"

Fritz reached in his vest pocket and took out a pack of cigarettes. He dug in the top of them until he pulled one out and put it to his lips. He patted his pockets, vest, and pants and then looked up at the officer. Buddy nodded, and the policeman lit his cigarette. Fritz blew a stream of blue smoke before fixing his gaze on Buddy.

"Taking care of business," Fritz said, and then looked away.

"What kind of business were you taking care of?"

"Stone business."

"That's why you shot this man? Tell me in your own words. I'm not going to help you say it. This is much too important for me to prompt you and pull every sentence out of you one word at a time. So you've got to talk."

"The Stone boy. He was shot. This man, this Drakos. He shot the boy. I shot him."

"How do you know he shot Harlan?"

"The paper. This morning."

"It never said he was guilty, Fritz. It said he was being questioned. Do you fully understand what you have done? This is attempted murder. Do you comprehend that?"

"Comprehend?"

"Understand. Do you understand what you have done?"

"Why do you think I can't understand? Because I do not speak good your language? This does not make me your dummy."

Buddy considered what Fritz had said and realized everyone in town talked down to this man for just this very reason. He studied Fritz's features in general and his eyes in particular and weighed his own words and his tone a little more carefully before he asked the next question.

"Fritz," Buddy said as he pulled up a chair across from him, "why did you walk in here this morning and shoot Nicoli Drakos?"

"For the Stones."

"For Harlan?"

"And H. V."

"H. V.'s been dead for twenty years."

"Dead does not matter. For H. V. And for the boy."

"You know I'm going to have to handcuff you and take you to jail. You're going to need a lawyer, and chances are you'll go to prison because of this."

"I'm ready."

Buddy waited for anything else the old man might want to add. But he could tell after a long interval that Fritz was through talking. He would have to undergo more questioning later, but for now there was very little need to badger the frail soul sitting in front of him. He motioned for the officer to handcuff Fritz and walk him out. As the policeman was guiding Fritz to the door, Buddy had one last question. "You got any family to be notified, Fritz?"

"A sister."

"Where is she?"

"I don't know."

Then the two men walked out the door. Buddy sat for a moment trying to understand it all.

CHAPTER FIFTY-NINE

Ellie was sitting on the sofa with her legs curled beneath her. She was leafing through the current Ladies' Home Journal while waiting for her favorite ten o'clock TV show. Matthew was in bed and Elizabeth was in her room, if not asleep. The house was quiet, and the den was in shadows from the one lamp that spilled light across her shoulder. Cal sat down on the ottoman and rubbed the head of their little cocker spaniel, Chester, who was sleeping on the floor.

"I got a call last week I haven't told you about," Cal said softly.

"I'm not surprised," Ellie said without looking up from her magazine.

"What's that supposed to mean?"

"Nothing. Go ahead."

"Buddy called me."

"Buddy Briggs?"

"It's the only Buddy I know," Cal said a little too quickly.

"Well, excuse me. I'll try not to interrupt."

"You've got to know it's about time for another move. We're beginning our fifth year here, and I'm sure I'll hear from the bishop before long. So anyway, Buddy called, and it looks like there's an opening back home."

"Mt. Jefferson?" Ellie asked as she met his eyes for the first time.

"Actually, the church I grew up in. They want me to come."

"And what have you decided to do?" Ellie asked, still leafing through the pages of the Journal.

"Well, I haven't decided anything. That's what I'm talking to you about."

"I think you should do whatever you want."

"You're comfortable with me making that decision alone?"

"Yes, Cal, as long as you're comfortable with me making my decision alone."

"I don't follow what you're saying."

"You don't want to follow what I'm saying. This is your chosen life, Cal. This is what you wanted from, I don't know when. Sometime in college. Well, you've got it, and I sincerely wish you well with it. I never knew exactly what attracted you to it, but then I guess that's none of my business."

"Of course it's your business."

"No, it's not. You and your big secret about what led you into this field. I've heard your friends back home ask you why. I've even heard Vic Princeton ask you, and you always squirm around and never tell anyone."

"That can't be what this is all about, Ellie."

"In a sense it is. You and your big secret in life."

"All I've ever said is that it was personal. It was a very personal experience, and when you make something that sincere and private …

when you make it public, you lose the sanctity of it. But if that's been eating at you all this time, I'll share it with you right now."

"No. Don't waste it on me, because I don't care. That's what I'm trying to tell you here. You make your decisions, and I'll make mine. And my plans, for me and the kids, do not include Mt. Jefferson."

"You mean if I move, you're not going with me?"

"Cal, I mean even if we stay, I'm not staying with you."

"How long have you felt this way?"

"I don't know. I didn't just wake up one day feeling like this. It comes on slow, with time."

"So, do you hate me or hate my life?" Cal asked with little love in his voice.

"I don't hate you. And I think very little about your life anymore, so I couldn't say I hate it. I'm just not interested. I have my own profession. I'd like to open my own accounting office someday. Maybe back in Louisville. And then the kids could have a home of their own and for once settle down and live a normal life."

"And if I took a job teaching somewhere, some college, what then?" Cal asked as a possible compromise.

"You're not going to do that, so don't try to fool me or yourself. You do what you've got to do. Just don't expect me to be a part of it."

Cal's heart filled with emotions he didn't know he could feel. His mind filled with pain he had never before felt. He felt paralyzed. Only his fingers were still functioning as he continued to stroke Chester's head. His thoughts went immediately to his children and what life would be without them each morning and each evening at suppertime. He could feel the pains in his chest at just the thought of being separated from them and not being there for all the little moments of their growing up.

And the church. The Mason Street Methodist Church. If he came home with no family, would they still want him? Did it show a lack of responsibility for a minister to be estranged from his family? Would this be such a bruise on his character that he would be more the center of gossip than the center of spiritual support? Could he even still be effective in the ministry as a divorced man of the cloth?

And then there was Chester. How he loved that little dog.

That was when it all started to come into perspective for James Calvin Vaxter. He was first concerned for his children; then the church; and then his dog. Ellie wasn't even in the top three. And maybe hadn't been for a long time.

Her career had always been more important to her than being a minister's wife. And why shouldn't it be? He understood her thinking; he just couldn't make himself agree with it. No congregation had ever warmed to her the way he wanted them to. Her heart and her time were just not in it. The members he hugged and greeted by first names each time he saw them were called Mr. and Mrs. by Ellie, and she only spoke to them when they spoke first. She attended none of the Bible studies he led, never consented to teach a Sunday school class, and constantly refused to help with the choir even though she was a terrific pianist and alto. She was more comfortable in the male-oriented world of public accounting and more content in a second-floor, windowless office than standing on the church steps beside him, shaking hands with old women and children. Maybe she was right. Maybe they both should make their own decisions.

He prayed about this twenty times a day. He talked to God and to his children with all the honesty his heart could afford. And then he decided it was time to talk to Buddy. He could start as early as April

1st. He had to laugh at the date. Maybe this was God's sense of humor, or maybe it was foreshadowing. Either way, he was ready for the next chapter of his life. Maybe there was a reason he was going home to Mt. Jefferson.

CHAPTER SIXTY

Nicoli was in surgery for two hours. It would be late afternoon before Buddy could talk to him. He used his time to send the twenty-two pistol off to Richmond for verification. He felt sure it wasn't the same gun that shot Harlan. He just couldn't imagine how that would make sense. He sat at his desk and sorted out his time frame for the day. He could go in and talk to Fritz again, but he knew in his heart it was a futile exercise. Fritz's reasons were—

"Lieutenant," Sergeant Tolley said from the doorway of his office. "Do you know that guy's last name?"

"I have no idea. I've never even thought of him having a last name. It's just been Fritz all my life. Check with Maxine at Stone's. She should know."

—simple and obvious. Fritz did what he did out of loyalty to the Stone family. He had been something to H. V. Stone from back in the beginnings of the store. Buddy had never really known their connection and relationship, and it had never been important until now. And even now he wasn't sure it was important. It was just a case of—

"Lieutenant, I got it. His last name is Corf," Tolley said.

"Corf?"

"That's what Maxine said."

"What kind of name is that?"

"I don't know. I always heard Stone wasn't really their name, either. It was Stoneheizer or something like that."

"Stonebrunner. But that has nothing to do with anything. And neither does Corf. Whoever he is or wherever he's from, it has nothing to do with what he did."

—old country loyalty. Looking out for your family. And the Stones were all the family he had. Except for that sister he'd lost track of. And how much could he blame the old man for? He wanted to blame Gary Akerman. He was the one who had set this whole thing up. Innocently, maybe. But that didn't make him less guilty. It just made him more—

"I'm sorry to bother you again, but Gary Akerman is out here and wants to see you." Tolley lowered his voice and said, "He looks like he's about to cry."

"Send him back."

The reporter came to the cubicle door with his straw hat in his hand. His face and his voice betrayed his tough-guy veneer. "Buddy, I don't know what to say. I'm just real sorry, and I'm ashamed of what I did. I even feel bad for Nicoli Drakos, and I never thought I'd say that, ever. I won't ever do anything like that again, I promise. I hear he's going to be all right. Is that true?"

"That's what they say."

"You know, Buddy, maybe I'm not cut out for this kind of work. I always thought I was but seeing the things I have to see and having to get in people's faces to draw a story out of 'em ... well, I just don't have the stomach for it. You know what I mean?"

Buddy sat silently at his desk and just shook his head slightly up and down so Gary couldn't be sure if that meant everything was okay or if Buddy was agreeing with him or dismissing him. Either way, Gary left before the tension got any thicker.

The next interruption came in the form of the phone ringing. The switchboard operator behind the front desk said he had an outside call from Harlan Stone. She connected them.

"Harlan."

"Buddy, what is going on down there?"

"You've heard, I guess."

"Only that Fritz shot Nicoli Drakos."

"Then you know as much as I do."

"Why would Fritz shoot Nicoli?"

"Are you still in the hospital?"

"Yeah. I may be going home tomorrow."

"Good. Maybe I'll know more of what to tell you by then."

"Why Nicoli?"

"It was in the paper this morning that I had him in here for questioning yesterday."

"Why?"

"Because I think there's a good chance he was the man who broke through your kitchen door and shot you in the side."

"Why would you think it was him?"

"Just some deductions I've made. Can you tell me for sure it wasn't him?"

"I'm pretty sure it wasn't."

"Even with that mask on?"

"Buddy, I think you're chasing the wrong dog."

"Did you call me to see what happened this morning or to talk me out of pursuing Nicoli Drakos?"

"What do you mean?"

"In case you're interested, ole Fritz is okay. He's doing just fine even though you haven't asked about him yet at all. The man who was willing to commit murder because of you. That's some pretty strong love, Harlan. And you haven't even asked about him. You're just concerned about Nicoli Drakos."

"I don't know what's got into you, Buddy, but I can't talk to you anymore."

"You could if you wanted to."

The dial tone rang in Buddy's ear.

CHAPTER SIXTY-ONE

It was 3:00 p.m. before Buddy got the call that Nicoli was out of surgery and able to talk. Buddy wasted no time getting to the hospital and to the designated room. A policeman was stationed outside the doorway, and a crowd of family was by Nicoli's bed when Buddy walked in. The mother and father, Nick and Christina; the brother and sister-in-law, Christopher and Sofia; and the sister, Korina in her nurse's uniform. The talk and tears that were being exchanged around the bedside came to a hasty halt when they spotted the cop in the room.

"I'm sorry for what's happened here. But if you don't mind, I'm going to need to talk to Nicoli alone," Buddy said firmly.

"What's happened here," Christopher said in a voice much too loud, "is that my brother was nearly killed this morning because you told some newspaper hack he was the man who shot Harlan Stone. That's what's happened here."

"Christopher," his mother said in a sad, soft voice, "don't make a scene."

"I'll do worse than make a scene. I'll show this …"

"Christopher," Nick said in a voice louder than his son's. "Your mother said don't make a scene. Now shut up. And let's leave while this man talks to Nicoli."

The family filed out, each looking Buddy in the eye as they passed. Buddy waited for them to leave and closed the door. He walked over to the bedside and sat on the closest chair.

"You feel like talking?" Buddy asked.

"No."

"Well, you're going to have to anyway. You know why you were shot this morning?"

"No. I was just sitting at my desk, and the door opened. Sandy, our secretary came in, I guess to tell me someone wanted to see me. But she barely got anything out of her mouth till in walked that little creep behind her. I thought he had come to look at a new apartment or something. It never once crossed my mind he was there to do me harm."

"Did he say anything?"

"Nothing. I said something like, 'What are you doing here, Fritz?' You know, just kind of surprised to see him in my office. He'd never been there before. And the next thing I knew he was pulling a gun out from under his vest and he shot me. Twice."

"What did he do then?"

"Just stood there. Sandy screamed and ran out the door. I started yelling for her to call the cops and call an ambulance. Fritz, he just went over in the corner and sat down on a chair and put the gun back in his vest."

"Were you conscious through it all?"

"Every hellish minute of it. I wish I *had* gone out. But there I sat holding my chest with blood running through my fingers. And there sat Fritz, crazy as a loon, just sitting there, looking at me."

"And you have no idea why he attacked you?"

"He thinks I shot his precious godson. So he's going to take me out for it."

"Nicoli, you got shot this morning with a twenty-two. Harlan got shot with a twenty-two. What do you make of that?"

"Coincidence."

"Reckon that's the twenty-two you said you lost?"

"I don't know. If I lost it, how would I know?"

"I can put you at the Stone house Wednesday morning. If I find that gun, I can put you away for a long time. But you play ball with me, and things will go easier."

"Look, Briggs. I'm hurting here. With every breath, I'm hurting. I know I've made a few mistakes, and I've made a mess of things. But I'm going to tell you something, and I ain't going to lie to you. I didn't shoot Harlan Stone."

"Even when I bring you proof of fingerprints you left in his kitchen?"

"That only proves I was there. Not that I shot him. Briggs, I swear on my mother's heart I didn't shoot him. I wish I had, but I didn't. And would you do me a favor?"

"What's that?"

"Would you get a nurse in here and see if they'll give me another shot of something. I'm hurting here, man. I'm hurting."

Buddy went directly back to the station. He motioned for Jim Tolley on the front desk to follow him back to his office.

"Jim, I need you to set up something."

"Name it, sir."

"I want you to put together a crew and search every ditch, creek, crevice, and trash can between Harlan Stone's house and Nicoli Drakos's house. Then search his office and his house."

"I'll need warrants."

"That shouldn't be hard to get now."

"What are we looking for?"

"A twenty-two–caliber pistol. He ditched it somewhere."

"Could it be the one that ole Fritz used on him this morning?"

"Not a chance. But speaking of Fritz, have someone bring him up. I have two questions I need to ask him. They're usually grateful and more talkative when they get out of the cell for a few minutes."

"Do you really think anything is going to loosen him up, Lieutenant?"

Chapter Sixty-Two

"Hello."

"Vic?"

"Yes."

"Are you alone?"

"I'm alone."

"I need to see you."

"You know I'm always here."

"If I come down the back alley, can I come in the back door?"

"There's nobody here but me. We just locked up, and everybody's gone home."

"I'll see you in a minute."

Vic walked to the back door that led out into the alleyway behind the restaurant. He slid the bolt and turned the lights off in the kitchen. The only light in the entire establishment was a sliver coming from the open door of his office and the tinted streams reflected in the floor tile from the neon sign out front. It gave an eerie and yet somehow warm glow to the place. You could see faces once your eyes adjusted to the dim light, but no one could see in from the outside. Vic knew this from experience. This wasn't the first time he had received an after-hours call.

In a few short moments the door pushed forward, and Christina Drakos came in and quickly shut it behind her. He took her hand, and they went to a darkened booth, where he poured them each a glass of wine.

"I guess you know about Nicoli," she said quietly.

"I know he's been shot and is in the hospital. How is he?"

"In pain. And that just breaks my heart."

"I know it does. I wish there was something I could do."

"There is, Victor. There is something you can do this time."

"What?"

"You can call off the police. They have hounded the boy until they got him shot, and now they still won't let him alone. Buddy Briggs was in his room today questioning him while he was lying there in so much pain he could barely see straight."

"But what do you think I can do?"

"If there is any one person in this town who has influence over Buddy Briggs, it's you. If you tell him to lay off and leave the boy alone, he'll do it. He'll do it for you."

"I don't think you know him very well, Christina. If he thinks he's doing the right thing, nothing will get in his way. And he's not going to be guided by the wishes of an old man trying to please his lover."

"Does he know?"

"No. None of them know."

"Do something, Victor. You owe me that."

"I owe you, Christina? You, who turned your back on me when we were in high school? You, who got married while I was away on tour? You, who wouldn't leave your husband because of some crazy loyalty even you don't understand? Don't tell me what I owe you, sweetie. I'd give you anything I have. Always would. Always will."

"Then try this time, please. Nicoli is innocent, and if only they will leave him alone, I think he can get his life back on the right track."

"Do you really think that? Or can you not just bring yourself to admit the boy just may not be any good? His environment has made him what he is. Face it, Christina. The boy's no good. It's not your fault. It just happened. He's no good."

"No, Victor. You don't believe that. Please do something. For the love of God, Victor, he's our son. Do something for him."

CHAPTER SIXTY-THREE

Bailey, the jailer, stepped in front of Buddy's open doorway.

"I've got him. Where do you want him?" Bailey asked.

"In here."

Bailey led Fritz to the straight chair in front of Buddy's desk. The little man sat down, keeping his gaze on the floor.

"Uncuff him," Buddy ordered.

"Are you sure?" Bailey asked.

"I'm sure. Uncuff him."

Bailey did as he was told and put the handcuffs and the key in his pocket. "You want me to wait on him?"

"No. I'll call you when I'm through."

And Fritz Corf and Buddy Briggs were alone in the small office.

"I didn't know your last name until today, Fritz. I apologize for that. All these years. I should have known that. We've never talked much, have we?"

Fritz kept his stare to the floor, occasionally rubbing his wrists where the handcuffs had chafed against his skin. Buddy got up

306   DON REID

and walked around the desk and into the hall. He stopped the first
uniformed policeman he saw.

"Do you smoke?"

"Sure. You want one?" the officer asked.

"No. I want the whole pack."

"What?"

"Just give me the whole pack. And give me some matches."

The patrolman reluctantly handed over a nearly full pack of
Camels to his superior officer without another word, and Buddy
went back to his office. He handed the cigarettes and matches to
Fritz and then sat back down at his desk.

"I have two questions to ask you, and then I'll leave you alone.
But I'll tell you before we start—I need you to talk to me. If you
want me to help you, I need you to give me information. Do you
understand?"

Fritz's only answer was two streams of smoke through his nose.

"When you shot Nicoli Drakos this morning, why didn't you
kill him? That's what you went there for, wasn't it?"

"No."

"You went there with a gun and you shot him twice in the chest,
but you never meant to kill him?"

"No."

"What did you mean to do?"

"Just what I did. Watch him suffer."

"That's it? That's all?"

"That's what he did to the boy. I wanted him to have the same."

"And if he had killed Harlan?"

"I would have killed him."

Buddy leaned back in his chair and studied the complex human being sitting across from him. There was either so much more or so much less to this man than he could fathom. It was hard to know where to come at him with each new question. Strategy was lost on him. And intimidation was impossible.

"Then I have one more question," Buddy said. "Where did you get the gun?"

"Why?"

"Because I have to know that."

"You know I shot the man. Why does gun matter?"

"I'm just asking for one more answer, Fritz. Don't play with me. Where did you get the gun?"

"Not mine."

"Then whose is it?"

"H. V.'s."

"H. V. gave you the gun twenty years ago?"

"No. He never gave it to me. It's his gun. Always kept one in the store. In a box under my table in the back. In case of robbery, I could get it quick. It was his gun. Still is."

"H. V. trusted you a lot, didn't he?"

"And I him."

"Do you trust Harlan?"

"He's good boy."

"He's in a lot of trouble. Did you know that?"

Fritz drew his mouth down, showing his disapproval at Buddy's judgment of Harlan.

"Did you know the store is in a lot of financial trouble, Fritz?"

"Not my business."

"You might be out of a job soon. Do you know all about that?"

"More than you do."

"Then tell me all about it. I think the trouble Harlan is in is related to why he was shot. If you know something I don't, it will help me prove who shot him and why. Do you know who shot him?"

"Drakos."

"Do you know why?"

Fritz stiffened again, and his frown gave him a dangerous and determined look.

"Fritz, is Harlan gambling at the Thursday night games with the Drakos boys and their crowd?"

"No."

"Are you sure?"

"The boy never gambles."

"You mean he is not in debt to the Drakos family?"

"I didn't say that."

"Talk to me, Fritz. What are you trying to tell me?"

"Store is in much trouble. No money to pay the bills. The boy gives all he can earn to the Drakos."

"Gambling debts, right?"

"Yes. But not his."

"Then whose?"

"H. V.'s."

Buddy sat back in his chair with his mouth open. For the first time, a few things were beginning to make sense.

"Are you telling me Harlan has been paying off H. V.'s gambling debts all these years?"

"And with much interest. He never gets out of the hole. H. V. gambled when he was sick. Lost it all."

"So Harlan's not gambling, but his daddy was. And Harlan's going broke trying to pay off Drakos with interest on the old man's debt."

"Don't say 'old man.' Say H. V."

"So Drakos shot him because he couldn't pay?"

"No."

"Why else would he shoot him then?"

"Sister Drakos. Beauty means more to the boy than money."

CHAPTER SIXTY-FOUR

Eight thirty-five, and the early summer evening had begun its descent into dusk as Harlan lay in the quiet of a lonely hospital room. The sheets below him were crumpled and uncomfortable, and the radio by his bed was filled with more static than song. But he had neither the desire nor the inclination to fix either annoyance. He just wanted to lie there and float through his misery. Someone knocked lightly on his open door. His quick glance to the doorway brought a smile to his face. "Cal, ole buddy, what are you doing here this time of night?"

"Night? You're too young to think of eight thirty as night. This is when you used to just start perking."

"Used to, yeah." Harlan laughed. "Do you remember when we used to go out on a Friday night just like this one and double date? And then after we took the girls home, we'd go back and lie in your front yard or mine and talk and laugh till sometimes two or three o'clock in the morning. You remember that?"

"Of course I do," Cal assured him. "And your daddy would stick his head out around midnight and say, 'You boys either quiet up out here or get yourselves to bed.' And we'd laugh even harder as soon as he'd close the screen door."

"Oh boy, do I remember that. My dad always wanted to appear a lot tougher than he really was. I think only you, and maybe Buddy, really knew what a big ole moon of a heart he had." Harlan closed his eyes for a second or two and reflected on what he had just said.

"I really liked your dad, Harlan. He was as good to me as he was to you. Did I ever tell you about the night I went to see him in the hospital during your wedding reception?"

"You left my wedding reception?"

"You didn't even miss me, did you?"

They both laughed.

"I took H. V. a piece of cake and a glass of punch, and he sat up in bed and ate it like he was starved. He was listening to the radio when I walked in just like you were just now."

"What did you two talk about?"

"We talked about a lot of different things," Cal said as he sat down on the side of Harlan's bed. "I know you remember the night I called you in New York to tell you he had passed. I wanted so badly to tell you some of those things that night, and I've meant to tell you a number of times since. But something always got in the way."

"I was lying here thinking about him just before you walked in."

"Did you ever know that he was bothered that Uncle Vic was your best man?"

"What do you mean bothered?" Harlan seemed shocked.

"A little jealous. And it wasn't just the wedding. I think he was jealous of Vic for a long time. He felt like Vic was trying to take his place with you. Trying to be a second father and he didn't need any help. And then there were other things."

"Like what?"

"He confided in me he was Jewish. I think he worked pretty hard to keep that a secret here in town. Yet he showed me that he knew the Bible. He had a pretty good knowledge of the New Testament, even. Were you aware of that?"

"Anything my dad did or knew never surprised me. The only thing that's ever surprised me is you telling me he was jealous of someone. That doesn't sound like H. V. Stone. And if you weren't the one telling me, I wouldn't believe it. But if you say so, I know it's true. What else did he tell you?"

"Oh, he asked me if I was going to get married. I told him I probably would. And at that time I thought it was the greatest thing in the world for me to do."

"Did he discourage you or urge you to do it?" Harlan asked.

"Neither one, really. But looking back, I wish someone had talked to me about it."

"It hasn't worked out very well for you, has it, ole pal?"

"No. And I really don't have anyone to blame but myself. I try to blame Ellie for it all. I tell myself she's not interested in my life and my profession. And even though she's not, that's not the whole problem. I'm not a good husband, Harlan. I'm not always there. In body, but not in mind and spirit. I'm not the most open human being alive. I'm not the easiest person to live with. When I get my mind on something, I'm like an old workhorse with blinders. I don't give much of what's inside me to the people who love me. I know all this but can't always do something about it. I know what to tell other people to do to help their lives and their marriages, but I can't seem to do the right thing to help my own."

The two friends of nearly four and a half decades sat in silence while the radio spit out an unrecognizable song. As much as two minutes passed before Cal spoke again. "But I came here to console you."

"And I wish I could do something for you and for Ellie."

"Don't worry about it. It'll all be right in time. I have faith that it will," Cal said as he stood up to leave.

"Before you go, anything else my dad say to you that night?"

Cal rubbed his nose and squinted as he tried to recall that particular moment so many years prior.

"Yes. I remember him asking me, 'Did you come here tonight to save my soul?'"

"And what did you tell him?"

"I don't save souls, Harlan. That's above my pay scale. Let's have a prayer before I go."

CHAPTER SIXTY-FIVE

Harlan was lying in his hospital bed on Saturday morning listening to the local news when his doctor came in the room. Without any greeting, Dr. Yandell took his chart from his bed rail and stood for a moment reading it. He looked up and smiled. "Well, you had a pretty good night, didn't you, Harlan?"

"I did. I feel better this morning than I've felt in years."

"Don't get *too* frisky, but I think you can go home today."

"I've been holding my breath for that."

"You'll still have some pain and you may have a little discharge from the wound from time to time, but keep it clean—and no straining of any kind. No lifting, no driving, no steps. Can you sleep on the first floor?"

"Darcy will make me a bed on the sofa downstairs. Just anything to get home."

"Okay. I'll have a nurse call her and tell her she can come pick you up anytime."

"When can I go back to work?"

"Come see me at the office Tuesday morning at ten. We'll talk about that then. But I expect you'll be ready by the next week."

"Thanks, Doc. You've really taken good care of me."

"Just see you that you take half that good of care of yourself. I know you, Harlan. You're not a nineteen-year-old stallion anymore. Take it easy."

Cal was in his study just off of the sanctuary at Mason Street Methodist. He was the only person in the church as far as he knew, so he jumped when he heard a knock on the office door.

"Come in," he called.

The figure that filled the doorway was the last person on earth he would have expected to see. He knew it must have shown all over his face when he stood up and extended his hand. "Nick Drakos. Come in."

"Preacher, how are you? Hope I'm not disturbing you."

"Not at all. Just catching up on a few odds and ends while I have a quiet moment."

"I won't keep you, but I wanted to speak to you privately."

"There's no one here but you and me and the Lord."

"I like that. I like that very much. And that's kind of why I'm here, Preacher."

Cal was annoyed by the way he used the word *preacher* as a name.

"Well, have a seat and make yourself comfortable."

"I don't go to church a lot anymore. I was raised in the church, understand. But through the years I've gotten away from it. Never took my boys and my girl the way I should. And I miss it. I miss that spiritual connection. Know what I mean?"

"Certainly. And you're always welcome to join us here anytime."

"I don't know. It's awkward now. It's been so long. But you never lose that need to share yourself with the Lord. To share the fruits of your success. I was brought up that way, and I've gotten away from it."

"I understand." He didn't, but he said he did for the rhythm of the conversation.

"Preacher, I'd like to give some money to this church. Would that be okay with you?"

"We've never turned any down before."

"And I hope you won't turn me down."

Nick Drakos laid an envelope on Cal's desk that was stuffed with cash. Cal inspected it without actually picking it up and saw it was full of fifty- and hundred-dollar bills. "That looks like a lot of money, Nick."

"Ten thousand dollars. And it's all yours."

"All the church's you mean."

"However you want to handle it, Little Cal. However you and Buddy want to handle it."

"Buddy? Buddy is a member of our administrative board, but he doesn't handle any of the finances."

"That's up to you, Preacher. You two can do with it what you please. As for me, I'm giving it to the Lord."

Cal leaned back in his chair, scratched his head, and smiled his warmest smile at the well-attired gentleman looking back at him.

But when he spoke, the coldness in his voice did not match the warmth in his face.

"Nick. I'm too sharp for your game. You can bring your money in the church and cleanse it, but I'm not fooled. You mention Buddy because you want him to know, through me, what a wonderful thing you have done here this morning. This is your substitute for the bribe to protect your son, the bribe you know he wouldn't take. Of course, you'll storm out of here and deny all this, but we both know what I'm saying is true. So I'll give you one chance to pick up your money and leave. But if you decide to leave without it, I'll keep it and make it clean for you. It will go to good mission causes and building repairs and children's community programs. Might even buy a new piano for the Fellowship Hall we're remodeling. But it will in no way affect anything that is happening in your family concerning the law. And if I were you, I'd stop worrying so much about the law and be a little more concerned about the grace."

Buddy waited till he saw the car leave the driveway. He walked up through the yard to the rear of the house and used the file on his fingernail clippers to open the back door. He quietly pushed it open and went inside.

CHAPTER SIXTY-SIX

Buddy was back at the station by 11:00 a.m. A call rang through for him just as he sat down at his desk.

"Briggs."

"Buddy, Cal here. I just heard from Harlan. He and Darcy are about to leave the hospital, and I'm going to meet them at their house and help him in. Just thought you might want to know."

"Sure. I was going over there anyway when he got home."

"I'll tell you about this later, but you'll never guess who came to see me at the church this morning."

"Animal, vegetable, or mineral?"

"None of the above. Nick Drakos."

"At church? Was he lost?"

"He came with a mission in mind. Bribery."

"How do you bribe a preacher?"

"It's easy if his best friend is a cop. I'll tell you all about it when I see you."

"Okay. See you in about an hour."

Darcy was standing at the sink, and Harlan and Cal were sitting at the kitchen table when Buddy knocked on the back door. The dog barked once, and Buddy went in.

"Well, you look like nothing ever happened," Buddy said to Harlan.

"I'm a little stiff, but boy, it sure is good to be home. Darcy's making lemonade and sandwiches. Want some?"

"No, thanks. I'll be real honest with you, pal, I didn't come over here on a hundred-percent friendly call."

The room went quiet, and all three fixed their eyes on Buddy. Before he could continue, Darcy spoke. "Buddy, Harlan just this minute walked into the house. Can't you give him a little rest before you light in on us again?"

"No. No, I can't, Darcy. I want to, but I can't."

"You want me to leave, Buddy?" Cal asked from his seat at the table.

"No. I want you to be here."

Harlan said nothing. He just sat intently, watching every move Buddy made. Buddy was standing in the center of the room and held his position as he began to talk.

"I think I know what happened here Wednesday morning. I'm going to ask you one more time to tell me."

"You've been told," Harlan spoke with anger biting every word.

"I've been told something, but not everything. I know Nicoli Drakos busted through that very door Wednesday morning. I'm not real sure of the time because I don't know how truthful you've been about that. It was probably earlier than you told me. And I also don't know if he was wearing a mask or not. I don't imagine he was because he wanted you to know it was him. He was here to scare you, Harlan. Scare you is all Nicoli has the stomach for. He carries that little peashooter to make himself feel like a big man, but he wouldn't have the guts to use it if he had an army backing him. And then I think you two fought. You took the gun away from him some way or another—maybe when you threw that chair at him, you overpowered him. But then he ran like the little coward he is, out the back door. And somebody else shot you, Harlan. Somebody besides Nicoli. He wasn't even here when it happened because if he knew, he'd love to tell me. But he doesn't know. Only you know. And … you."

Buddy turned when he said this and looked directly at Darcy, who was still standing at the sink with an empty glass in her hand. The glass fell and shattered at her feet, and she slowly bent double and gave out a long, shrill cry that sounded like it came from a wounded animal. Cal went immediately to her to help her up and into a chair, but she ignored his efforts and stayed on the floor on her knees.

"I can tell you," she screamed through her tears. "I can tell you what you have to know! Why won't you leave us alone? But I know you won't! So yes, I can tell you what you want to hear, Buddy Briggs!"

She paused to catch her breath and wipe her face with her hand and leaned her head heavily against the cabinet doors. Harlan was looking not at her but at his hands, which were gripping each other in his lap.

"We heard the door being kicked in and we both ran down the steps and found him—Nicoli Drakos—standing right there where you're standing now. He had a horrible look on his face, and I was scared. More scared than I've ever been in my life. Harlan said something to him, and he said something back. I can't really tell you what they said because all I could see was the gun he had in his hand. And I knew he was going to shoot us. The only thing I heard for sure was, 'Stone, stay away from my sister. If I ever catch you with her, I'll slit your throat.' Then I saw a chair fly across the room. Harlan had thrown one of the kitchen chairs at him. It knocked Nicoli back against the sink, and he dropped the gun. Harlan lunged for him, and I grabbed the gun. Nicoli ran. He went out the back door, and we let him go."

"That's enough, Darcy. You've said enough." Harlan spoke from his stupor.

"Tell me the rest of it," Buddy insisted.

"Shut up, Darcy!" Harlan yelled.

Buddy reached in his coat pocket and pulled out a small black twenty-two pistol and walked over and placed it on the table.

"Where did you get that?" Darcy asked with more panic in her face.

"From the sock drawer in your bedroom. It's been dusted for prints. It's been identified. And in forty-eight hours it will be matched to the bullet that shot your husband over here. No doubt in my mind. And none in yours either, Darcy."

"You said you were going to get rid of it," Harlan yelled.

"I meant to. Oh, I'm so sorry. I meant to," Darcy cried.

"Go on, Darcy. Finish your story," Buddy demanded.

"We were both left standing here in the kitchen, and all I could hear ringing in my head was, 'Stay away from my sister.' I asked Harlan what that meant, and like always, he started in on a big long lie. I had just heard it too many times, and while he was rattling off one lie after another, I realized there was a gun in my hand. And I could see Korina

Drakos and how beautiful she is and fifteen years younger than me and I was so mad I wanted to scream. And I shot him. Just that simple. I shot him. And I wasn't even sorry. I liked finally having some control over him. But then seeing him lying there on the floor, I felt sorry for him and knew I still loved him. So I called the ambulance, and while we were waiting, we made up the story we were going to tell."

"How did you find this gun, Briggs?" Harlan asked, spitting out each word.

"I came in here this morning and searched your house."

"You broke in? Then this evidence is tainted. You can't prove anything 'cause you got this gun illegally."

"Calm down, Harlan," Buddy said as he walked to the table and put the gun back in his coat pocket. "Do you have any idea what you two have done? You, Darcy, have shot your husband. And in doing so have caused another man to commit attempted murder on an innocent person. Can you see everything you've caused by your actions and by covering up your actions?"

"I'm sorry." She began to sob uncontrollably. "I'm so sorry. I'm so sorry."

"You can't let this go any further, Buddy. Please," Harlan begged.

"Just a second ago it was Briggs. It's back to Buddy now that you want something?"

"I want nothing for me, Buddy. I want it for Darcy. You can't turn her in. I won't press charges. You can't turn her in."

"I don't need you to press charges. I can handle that myself. This woman is a danger to herself and her family."

"No, Buddy. I love her. It was all my fault. It was all my fault. Please," Harlan continued to plead.

Cal was on the floor on his knees, trying to calm and console Darcy as her sobs grew more violent.

The phone in the den rang. And then again.

"Let it ring," Harlan said. "I don't care who it is."

"I do," Buddy said. "The station knows where I am. It might be for me."

"Then you answer it," Harlan said. " I don't want to talk to anybody."

Buddy walked into the quieter den and answered the phone on the fifth ring.

"Stone residence. Briggs speaking."

"Buddy? Is that you?" Amanda asked on the other end of the line.

"Yeah."

"What are you doing answering the phone? Is everything all right?"

"Yeah, honey. Long story. What's up?"

"I called the station. They said I could find you there. Buddy, you're a grandpa!"

"Really?"

"I'm at the hospital now."

"Why didn't somebody call me?"

"There was no time for them to call anybody. It all happened so quickly, Louis Wayne just barely had time to get her in the car. She didn't even make it all the way in the hospital. The baby was born in the parking lot of the emergency room. On the front seat of the car. Louis Wayne and a nurse, who ran outside to help, delivered it. You know that nurse from the other night? The real pretty one—Korina? She and Louis Wayne delivered your grandson."

"A boy, huh? How about that."

EPILOGUE

Buddy and Amanda ate dinner with Cal and Vic at Mulligans in the back booth on the right. They were just finishing dessert as twilight was settling over Main Street and Mt. Jefferson was preparing for a hot summer night.

"So you think he looks like Buddy?" Vic asked.

"I really do. He has his chin. And all that wavy brown hair." Amanda was still floating from the excitement of the day even with all the sadness and disappointment that tried to crowd it out.

"That's silly," Buddy said. "A baby doesn't look like anybody. It just looks like a little wrinkled baby. He won't take on real features till he's at least a year old. *Then* he'll look like me."

They all laughed and then climbed out of the booth. The four walked to the front together. Vic kissed Amanda good night, and she and Buddy walked up the street toward the police station, where their car was parked.

Cal and Vic stood at the front of the nearly empty restaurant and watched them as they went arm in arm.

"I stayed with Darcy and Harlan for a long time this afternoon," Cal said. "Then I realized Buddy was in just as much pain as they were, so I left and found him. I've never seen three more anguished people in my life. But I'm so happy for Buddy and Amanda. It's been a real rough day. But all things will pass, and when they look back on this one I hope they can only remember it as their grandchild's birthday. And just bury all the bad memories."

"Yeah, I guess. But you know, it's the things we bury inside that makes us old. We all have our sins, and we all have our secrets," Vic said, looking out at the street.

"You got secrets?"

"Oh, my boy—you have no idea."

Cal looked over at him and said, "Don't be too sure, Uncle Vic. Anytime you need to talk, you know I'm here."

Vic said nothing but firmly clasped his hand on the younger man's shoulder. Cal smiled and looked back out the window.

"What do you think Buddy will do about Darcy? Is he going to take her in or let her go?"

"Don't you worry about Buddy, son. One thing you can count on is that he will always do the right thing. He's a good man, and he'll do the right thing."

... a little more ...

When a delightful concert comes to an end,

the orchestra might offer an encore.

When a fine meal comes to an end,

it's always nice to savor a bit of dessert.

When a great story comes to an end,

we think you may want to linger.

And so, we offer ...

AfterWords—just a little something more after you

have finished a David C Cook novel.

We invite you to stay awhile in the story.

Thanks for reading!

Turn the page for ...

- **An Interview with the Author**
- **Discussion Questions**
- **Acknowledgments**

An Interview with

the Author

This is your second book set in the town of Mt. Jefferson. What made you want to return to this town?

I like these people, and there were more I wanted to introduce. More merchants, friends, and lives to crisscross. This town is peaceful to me. I'm lost on the streets and in the shops and in the era and hope the reader is lost in there with me. It was a time of no cell phones, no satellites, and no home computers. It was one-car families and black-and-white TV. I love the simplicity of the times.

The friendship between Cal, Harlan, and Buddy is a vital part of this story. Did any of your relationships inspire aspects of theirs?

Oh, yes. I grew up with some close friends, and we explored the streets of our small town when we were kids. I grew to adolescence with those friends and then to manhood. Some are still with me, but one is gone. But when I can go back to Mt. Jefferson, then I have them all together again.

Which character surprised you the most as you wrote this story?

Buddy Briggs. I thought I knew him best, but he kept surprising me. I saw the side he showed his wife and daughter; then the side he showed his friends. And then I saw just how hard he could be in his job. It brought out the dimensions I wasn't sure of until I saw them on the paper myself. He's hard when he has to be, and when Cal and Darcy saw his business side, I think they were as surprised as I was.

Which of the characters was most difficult for you to write, and why?

Harlan. I wanted him respectable yet flawed. Lovable but not always likable. I wanted the reader to be on his side but still to understand he wasn't a perfect human being by any measure.

What surprised you most about the story line as it evolved?

The relationship between Vic and the three Mulligans. Even though I knew where I wanted to go, I couldn't have told you for sure on the first day of writing just how their adult relationship was going to be in the end. I love where it took me and love who Vic was and who he became to the boys. He's a hero of sorts to them, and he is to me also. He's like a couple of favorite uncles of mine. The kind you can entrust with boyhood secrets and feelings.

How would you describe the role of faith in *The Mulligans of Mt. Jefferson?* The role of family?

The role of faith is the simple old second-chance philosophy of the New Testament. Peter asked Jesus, "How many times shall I forgive my brother? Seven times?"

And Jesus said, "No. Seventy times seven."

That's a lot of second chances. You do the math, and you'll find it staggering.

As for family, we see the warmth and problems in Buddy's family; the stress and separation in Cal's; the pressure and expectations in Harlan's. We see in these families all the good and bad we see in our own and our friends' and neighbors'. I think just seeing it on paper and knowing it happens to others makes our own daily bumps in the road a little easier to absorb.

What do you hope readers will take away from the story?

Second chances. Friendships. Family ties. Loyalty. Hard decisions. Comfort of God in doing the right thing.

Discussion Questions

1. What was your first impression of the main characters in this story? What surprised you most about the development of those characters as the story went on?

2. Which character could you relate to the most and why? Which of the characters' struggles and imperfections resonated with you?

3. What did you find most intriguing about the 1959 story line? About the boys' growing-up years?

4. We see several examples of family relationships shaping the characters. How did these relationships positively or negatively impact the main characters over the course of their lives?

4. Buddy, Harlan, and Cal experienced different struggles and joys in their individual marriages. Which relationship could you relate to the most?

5. What role did Mulligans play in the story? How did Vic's friendship shape Buddy, Harlan, and Cal?

6. What story element made you most uncomfortable? What encouraged you the most?

7. What role did faith play in the lives of the main characters?

ACKNOWLEDGMENTS

How long does it take you to write a book?

Where do you get your ideas?

Is it lonesome working all by yourself?

These are just a few of the FAQs I, and all book writers, get. And to be honest, they're pretty good questions. I don't always have a good answer for them, but they're good questions.

I have never learned how to compute that first one. One doesn't sit down and begin writing and never get up from his chair until it's finished. There are so many interruptions and distractions—some lasting for hours—some lasting days and weeks. So to try to figure how long it would have taken if one had the luxury of staying at it with no phone calls, visitations, appointments or lazy days—well, I just don't know where to start the clock.

As for the second one, it has multiple answers. Daydreams, memories, conversations, failures, accomplishments. You draw from all things good and bad you have experienced or not experienced in life and roll them into a tale from which you hope someone will get a sense of enjoyment or inspiration. If they get both, you've got a winner.

But number three is much easier to answer. You never work all by yourself. There are many who have a hand in the work it takes to put a book together. And here are a few of the best:

Mary Sue Seymour, my agent, deserves my first and sincerest thank you. She's a sweetheart and a professional of the highest order. And she's a good friend.

Don Pape heads up the publishing side and decides who's going to print and who isn't. Truly, without him there is no book.

Steve Parolini has edited three manuscripts for me. He quietly makes me look good; like I know what I'm doing even when I don't. I wish I knew all he knows.

Ingrid Beck is in charge of Artist Relations. She holds our hands, hears our gripes, and fixes our problems. And does it all with such grace.

Michelle Webb gets the books to me and sees that all the orders are correct and accounted for. Without her I'd have nothing to sign and you'd have nothing to read.

Caitlyn York, the last editor before the release, is a strict one. She holds my feet to the fire. She picks up the little things writers sometimes drop in the rush of the moment. She's got a great eye and ear for what's right.

And then there's my proofreaders—my wife, Debbie; brother Harold; sons Langdon and Debo. They give me good feedback. They tell me what they like and what they don't care for. I trust them as much as I love them.

So how long does it take to write a book? About four months.

Where do I get the ideas? Somewhere in that area between heart and mind.

Is it lonesome working all by yourself? I'd be scared to try.

Don Reid
August 1, 2011
7:40 p.m.